BEAUTY & THE BOY

BEARYTALES
BOOK SIX

SUE BROWN

BEARYTALES #6

1

Alec Brenner stared at the piece of paper, a single sheet with a short paragraph.

"This can't be real."

"I'm sorry, Brenner. It's true."

The slender man who'd just detonated his life gave him a pitying look. Somehow that made it worse. No one wanted Josh Cooper to feel sorry for him because then you knew it had to be serious.

Cooper had insisted on traveling to meet them. It was a gesture they appreciated. Cooper was supposed to be based in London, but since the Kingdom orphanage horror had broken, he spent as much time in Angel Securities' office in Seattle, as he had across the Atlantic.

Beside him, Jake, Alec's younger brother and his business partner in the private investigator firm, shifted restlessly on the couch in their office. "Does Matt know?"

Cooper huffed. "I don't know. I think he suspects, but

we won't know for sure until you have that conversation with him."

"Me!" Alec stared at him, horrified.

"Who else?" Cooper spread his hands in a gesture that told Alec that he needed to man up or else.

"He's your boy," Jake said quietly beside him.

"He's not my boy," Alec snapped, "and that's his choice, not mine."

Jake gripped Alec's bicep. "He's your boy in every way that matters, big brother, and you must be the one to give him the news. There's no one else he'll hear it from. I'll be right beside you when you do. You don't have to do this alone. And the family will back you up."

Alec gave him a bleak look. "Will they? Will Lyle and Vinny back me up? Will Gruff and Damien, once they know? You know how they feel about Kingdom Mountain."

Jake's flinch was enough. "It's gonna be hard on all of us," he admitted. "But we've faced everything as a family, and we'll face this together too."

As Alec crumpled, Jake wrapped his brother in his arms and held him tight.

Josh Cooper got to his feet. "I'll leave you alone for a moment. I'm going back to the motel to talk to my husband and remind him I'm still alive. Find me when you're ready. There's one thing you need to think about, Alec. The Feds are going to want to talk to him. I can't hold them away for long. Forty-eight hours at the most."

Jake grimaced. "It's Lyle's birthday weekend."

"Vinny will kill me, then you, if you ruin his surprise party," Alec muttered.

Cooper snorted, then sighed. "I'll hold them off until after that. Let the family have their time in peace."

"Thanks, Josh," Jake said, not letting go of Alec for one moment.

Alec shuddered as the door closed and stayed where he was, his cheek pressed to Jake's soft sweater. "This is going to crush him."

"Matt's whole life has been one long struggle. This is just one more blow in an endless list of them." Jake didn't point out that all their boys had tragic lives until they met their Brenner brother. He didn't need to. "He'll survive because you'll be there to protect him."

Sitting up and wiping his eyes with a tissue, Alec tried to get himself together. Jake and Cooper were right about one thing. He was the only one who could tell Matt.

"I'll tell him when we get home." Alec rubbed his temples, trying to ease the start of a headache. If it caught hold it would lay him low and he didn't have time for that.

"We'll drive back tonight. Josh can come back with us if he wants."

They'd not been planning to return until the next day for a family dinner, but this was too important to wait. Although Matt didn't live with him and the Brenner household, the boys had invited him to stay, for a boys-only night, no Daddies allowed. They were taking over one of the new cabins to have fun.

Alec caught Jake's pinched expression. "What's wrong?"

Jake huffed, but he didn't speak. He seemed to be processing how he was going to deliver the news. Alec waited patiently, knowing his brother would tell him in his own time, even as his stomach churned. Alec wanted to yell at him to spit it out and deliver the bad news before he was too crushed to deal with it.

"Alec, there's something else you need to think about.

Cooper has only alluded to it, but if Matt knew what was going on, then he could be facing a lengthy prison sentence," Jake said.

Alec stared at his brother, horrified by what he was saying. "Matt was a victim. Just as much as Lyle or Vinny. You know that. Lyle told us."

Jake shrugged. "Maybe, but he survived, unlike hundreds of others."

"What are you saying?"

"I'm saying you need to prepare yourself, and him, for what lies ahead."

Alec stood, stalking over to the window, and stared out. In the distance, he could see Kingdom Mountain and if he squinted hard, he could believe he saw the twinkling lights at the end of their driveway that had been used to welcome the family home after weeks away dealing with the Kingdom boys. Now the lights were always on whenever one of the brothers was away from home. In this instance he and Jake. His older brother, Damien, complained about the cost, and still, the tree lights shone to welcome home family.

Jake joined him at the window. "Whatever happens, Matt's got a family who loves him."

"He should have stayed away from us...me. He used to be so happy," Alec said bitterly.

"Was he happy or was it a mask to hide how scared he was?"

Alec flicked a glance at his brother. "What do you mean?"

"The only time I see Matt truly happy is when he's leaning against you."

Alec said nothing and returned his gaze to the mountain. Matt did a lot of leaning, but not in Alec's arms. Oh, he and Matt fucked all the time. They'd been fuckbunnies as Matt called them, for longer than even Lyle had been in the family. As far as Alec knew, Matt wasn't seeing anyone else. During the dark days away, Matt hid in Alec's arms when he needed comfort. And Alec only had to call, and Matt would be there, grumbling all the while, but he would be there, for his Daddy Bear.

Matt spent more time working for Jake and Alec than he did at his own job at a local real estate firm. He didn't know, at least Alec had never told him, that he still had the job because Alec did PI work for free for his employer. He insisted he wanted a life away from the Brenners and Alec, and yet he always crept back to them. Who was he hiding from? Himself? His past? Or the authorities?

"I need to go home," Alec said abruptly.

Jake patted his arm. "You go. I'll deal with Cooper and follow you up later."

"Thanks." Alec leaned against Jake who gave him a one-armed strong hug. "You're getting a bear belly," he muttered.

"I know." Jake grimaced. "Aaron's developed this obsession with baking for me. I think he's struggling to know what to do with himself. It's not good for my waistline."

"You can always pass the cakes onto me."

"He's not brave enough to launch them onto the family. To be honest that's a good thing. They're hit and miss," Jake confessed, then he grimaced. "Probably more miss. He needs practice. I keep telling him to talk to Lyle and Vinny."

"Matt can't cook," Alec admitted. "He worked with the horses, not in the kitchens. I'm a better cook than he is and that's not saying much."

"Go home, Alec." Jake squeezed him again. "Be with your boy. He's gonna need you."

Alec's mind raced with the idea of men dragging his boy away from him. He replayed that image over and over, his boy screaming that he needed his Daddy. Matt's arms outstretched, reaching for Alec, and Alec being held back by his brothers, as black-clad, faceless men threw his boy into a windowless van and drove him away, leaving Alec distraught.

"I don't know what I'd do if they took him away from me," Alec said brokenly. "He's my life."

"We won't let them take him away. But first, he needs to know that you have discovered his dirty little secret."

"Hey, don't say that," Alec snapped. "Don't speak about my boy like that."

"I'm sorry," Jake apologized. "That came out all wrong."

Alec grunted. He knew his brother was sincere in his apology. He took a deep breath and stared up at the mountain. It would be well over an hour before he got home. Not for the first time he dreaded driving the long winding mountain road.

"How am I going to tell my boy I know his father is the CEO of Kingdom Mountain Theme Park, the man who started this horror-fest off?"

Jake squeezed his shoulder. "I don't know, brother. I don't know. But I'll be here for you. We all will."

MATT

Coming up to the cabin for a boys' night had been a mistake. It wasn't that Matt George didn't like the boys. He did. He even liked prickly Red who was settling into the family now, although it had taken time for him to relax with everyone. It wasn't that they didn't treat Matt as part of the family because they did, although he spent a lot of time running away. He walked in and out of the cabin as though he lived there.

Matt never intended to return to the Brenner home, but the ache for Alec and the family would get too much and he'd find himself parked in front of the cabin without any real knowledge of how he got there. He'd walk in to find the brothers and their boys around the table. Alec would pull a chair next to him and he'd be there, joining in, a cup of hot chocolate in one hand, and Lyle putting a plate of something delicious in front of him. The cabin was home. Alec was home. Matt just didn't want to admit it.

No, the problem was he had to face five couples in love every single time. Five Daddies cooing over their boys and five boys who loved their Daddies. They treated Matt like he was one of them. Alec treated Matt like his boy, therefore Matt must love Alec. They didn't ask, they just assumed.

The only one who didn't assume anything was Brad, the only brother who was unattached, and that was because he was mainly in the barn blowing shit up.

Matt loved Alec. Loving Alec had never been the problem. Matt just didn't want to face the monster in the room.

All of this went through Matt's head between parking his truck, picking up the pretty wrapped box, and walking into the large kitchen.

"Matt."

Vinny squealed and rushed over to hug him. Matt put down the box on the counter, caught the smaller man in his arms, and hugged him tight.

"You turned up," Vinny gasped. "I didn't think you would."

"I told you I'd be here when you phoned me the last three times," Matt pointed out.

Vinny leaned back to lock gazes with him. "You don't come here so much these days."

Matt pressed his lips together. Vinny had a point. He had deliberately stayed away. He forced a smile. "We're celebrating Lyle's birthday. I wouldn't miss it."

He stepped away from Vinny and bent down to scratch Vinny's dog, Rexy, behind the ears. Rexy closed his eyes and thumped his hind leg in ecstasy.

Lyle hadn't celebrated his birthday properly since he arrived at the cabin. His eighteenth birthday could have been the day he died, but instead, he was found unconscious in the snowy forest by a gay Daddy bear and his life and that of many boys like him changed forever.

Vinny had received presents on his eighteenth and he'd gotten the best present ever, his own Daddy. But Lyle's promised day never happened because they were too busy. His nineteenth birthday came and went as he was on the road, so his Daddy Gruff had put his foot down and said that for his twentieth, they were staying at home. Lyle was having a party, a family dinner he didn't have to cook, and lots of presents.

"Where's the birthday boy?" Matt asked, noticing Lyle wasn't in the kitchen.

"Gruff has taken him for a ride on Maggie. It was something they did when he first arrived," Vinny said, pulling a face.

Matt chuckled. Vinny's antipathy to horses was well known. Even the sweet nature of Gruff's placid old mare wasn't enough to make him change his mind.

"Are we all ready for tonight?" he asked.

Vinny nodded. "We're having a boys' party in my cabin tonight and then the big family meal tomorrow in here."

Matt squinted at him. "Are you sure you want us in your cabin? What if we spill something?"

Vinny waved his hand dismissively. "We're the only ones who haven't moved in yet. There's nothing to damage."

"Shouldn't you guys get this place as Damien is the oldest?"

"I wanted somewhere small just for us," Vinny said. "I've never had anywhere private to live. I can't imagine a home for just the two of us." He sounded almost awed at the thought.

It was a standing family joke that what Vinny wanted, Vinny got. His Daddy would walk through fire to make his boy happy. But of all of them, Vinny had been to hell and back all his life, brutalized by the Greencoats. They would *all* walk through fire for him, including Matt.

"It's strange to have privacy after the life we led," Matt agreed. He'd been a Kingdom Mountain boy too, although he'd been shipped to another theme park when he was younger.

"I can't wait. Red and Harry are so happy now."

"That leaves Alec and Brad in here?" Matt asked.

"Plus Lyle and Gruff. Their cabin isn't finished yet. I think Lyle loves this place and he's been delaying the inevitable."

"Hey, Matt," Aaron said from the doorway to the hall.

He, Jack, and Red appeared. As the newest of the boys and not from Kingdom Mountain theme park but one in Florida, they'd formed a clique of their own. They were also a little older than Lyle and Vinny, although Aaron's actual age was suspect. He talked about Rapunzel years a lot and Matt knew he wasn't as old as his driver's license said.

Aaron came over and kissed Matt on the cheek. "Glad you're here."

Matt hugged him and then squinted as he caught sight of what Red was holding. "Do you have balloons?"

It was a rhetorical question as the three helium-filled balloons filled the doorway.

"We do." Jack grinned. "Me and Red went to that new store in town. The one near the Tin Bar. Red found all these balloons and they had one for twenty and a Snow White balloon."

Matt held back an eye roll. There was a standing joke in the family that each brother and his boy were a fairy tale couple. Thankfully there was nothing that could be applied to him and Matt.

"What's the heart one for?" he asked.

"Gruff asked me to buy that one," Red said hastily. "It's nothing to do with me."

Like any boy would declare their love for someone else. They were all madly loved up. Except him, Matt thought sadly. He just couldn't take the dive over the edge of the mountain and commit to his Daddy Bear.

"What are you gonna do with them?" he asked, trying to push away the sad thoughts.

"I'm taking them to my cabin before Lyle gets back," Red said.

"I'm going with him to keep a lookout for Lyle," Jack said.

"Which leaves me with nothing to do," Aaron grinned.

"You two can help me get the food and drink to my cabin," Vinny informed him. "It's all ready."

Matt often thought Vinny should have been a general in another life. He was very good at giving orders. "Has Lyle guessed about his birthday surprise?"

"Nope!" Vinny sounded gleeful. "It's a total surprise."

Matt happened to catch the flicker in Aaron's eyes. That was more like it. Lyle was the heart of the Brenner household. Of course, he knew. But Lyle would never spoil the surprise for his best friend and brother, Vinny. He had a huge heart.

The kitchen door opened, Vinny squeaked, and Matt expected Lyle to walk through the door. But it wasn't the birthday boy. It was Alec. As far as Matt knew, Alec and Jake were staying in town overnight as they had a meeting with Josh Cooper.

Matt cocked his head and fixed his gaze on Alec. "What are you doing here, Daddy Bear? I thought you had a meeting with Cutie Pie?"

Normally Alec would scowl at the nickname for Cooper, but as he saw the muscles clench in Alec's jaw, Matt had a sudden sinking feeling he wasn't going to like whatever Alec had to say.

"Alec." Vinny scowled at him. "You're not about to ruin my party, are you?"

2

ALEC

It was a fair question and Alec really hoped he wasn't about to be proved a liar. He shook his head. Josh Cooper promised him forty-eight hours. He'd call Cooper and make sure he didn't renege on that. The family deserved two days to have fun without more drama. They deserved two decades, but he'd take what he could get.

"I didn't want to be away from the fun," he said lightly. "You promised a party. You know we Brenners love party time." He gave a wiggle as if he were pretending to dance. Out of the corner of his eye, he caught Matt's squint. Someone knew him well enough to know he was lying.

But fortunately, Vinny didn't seem to notice. He waggled a finger at Alec. "You stay with the brothers in here. Your turn is tomorrow. This is just the boys tonight. We're gonna have a great time."

Alec thought they could party with their Daddies who could be around to protect them, but he wasn't going to argue with Vinny. "I promise to stay away." He leaned around Vinny to look at Red. "Do you want Lyle to see those? Because he's on his way back."

"Shit." Red turned on his heel and headed for the boot rack.

"Dollar," Vinny called after him.

"Later!" Red grumbled as he disappeared.

"Tell Harry," Alec advised. "He'll pay up."

"It's time we started filling the swear jar again," Aaron said. "It was a good Thanksgiving."

It had been. A period of calm after the past two years. The meal was amazing, thanks to a full swear jar and Lyle's and Vinny's cooking. And the high point for Alec had been Matt coming into his arms and spending the holiday with him willingly.

Matt spent more time with him than not, yet he still wouldn't commit. But none of that mattered now, because Alec was about to turn his life upside down again. Alec just wanted to grab his boy and run with him, far away from Kingdom Mountain, from the authorities and Greencoats, to keep Matt safe.

"What's wrong?" Matt said, his voice low. "And don't say nothing because I'm not stupid, Alec. It's written all over your face."

Alec wanted to correct him, to demand that Matt called him Daddy, but he would never do that. Matt called him Daddy Bear instead, as a joke. Alec didn't want it to be a joke.

"I need to practice my poker face," Alec quipped. Matt scowled at him, and Alec sighed. "We need to talk soon."

"Where're you going?" Vinny asked, regarding them with a frown. "I need Matt to help me with the food."

Aaron came over to nudge Vinny. "I'll help you."

"We'll be back very soon," Alec promised. "I just need to talk to Matt. He'll be back for your boys' celebration."

"He'd better," Vinny said fiercely. "Or I'm coming to get him."

Alec hoped Matt would stay, for Lyle, otherwise the family wouldn't forgive Alec for screwing up. He glanced out of the corner of his eyes to see Matt trying to hide his apprehension. He was nervous about whatever Alec was going to say.

"I'll hide your gift with the others." Aaron loped over to take the present on the counter.

"I'd forgotten about that," Matt said.

"No problem."

Aaron, Jack, and Vinny vanished, leaving Matt staring at Alec.

Matt folded his arms. "So?"

"This conversation can wait," Alec suggested.

"No, it can't." Matt leaned forward. "If you're gonna wreck my weekend, I want to know why."

Alec huffed, knowing it was a lost cause. "Let's go for a walk."

Matt still wore his jacket and boots. He jammed his hat in his pocket and followed Alec out of the door. Alec idly noticed it was a well-worn old jacket of his from one of the trunks in the attic. Matt had declared he didn't want to wreck his good clothes on the farm, but Alec thought he just wanted to wear his Daddy's clothes like the other boys did but wouldn't admit it.

They stepped onto the verandah. This late in the year it was almost dark. The promise of snowfall hung in the air. Later on, the sky would be a deep, inky blue, the stars twinkling in the night sky. But now it was as if the world was holding its breath between the day and the night. Or maybe that was just the way Alec felt. This was the calm before the storm.

The thick snow crunched under their shoes as Alec led them down the stoop to a path that led to the barns and beyond. The chill of the winter breeze would be easier to handle amidst the comforting effect of the pine trees. They walked in silence, but finally, Matt grabbed Alec's arm.

"This is far enough. Tell me what it is. You're freaking the hell outta me, Alec."

Alec stopped and turned to face him, shoving his hands in his pockets because he'd left his gloves back in the truck. He had no idea how to say this, knowing it was going to destroy the man he loved.

"Before I say anything, I need to hold you. Please."

He held out his arms. Matt eyed him warily, then stepped in for a hug. Alec felt the tension in Matt before he relaxed, and his arms came around Alec's waist to hold him. Alec rested his cheek on Matt's hair. It felt soft as if he'd just washed it, rather than full of product as it usually was.

"Kiss me?" he begged.

Matt sighed but he reached up and they exchanged kisses. Alec kept it soft and chaste and brief, tasting the wintergreen on Matt's breath from the gum he kept in his truck. Then he stepped back and ran a hand through his hair.

"Talk to me, Daddy Bear," Matt pleaded. "You're really scaring me."

Alec gave a curt nod. "Cooper says the Feds are gonna want to talk to you soon."

Matt wrinkled his brow. "Me? Why? I thought our part was done."

"It is, but they've uncovered some news they need to talk to you about."

"Me?" Matt looked genuinely confused and Alec began to have hope for the first time since Cooper had dropped the bombshell that morning. Maybe this had all been a misunderstanding. There had been mistakes before, that had taken time to unravel.

He hesitated but then launched into his question. He couldn't delay it any longer. They were going to freeze if they stood out here much longer. Besides, it was going to snow. Alec could smell it in the air.

"Matt, sweet boy, do you know who your father is?"

Alec was watching for something, anything, and he saw it. He was a PI, he'd spent years watching his marks for the slightest reaction. He saw Matt flinch, his eyes go wide, and his fists clench, even as he tried to hide it. Alec rocked back on his heels, feeling as if he'd taken a blow to his gut. It took a moment before he could speak again.

"You know," he accused harshly and then tried to moderate his tone. "You know who he is."

Matt shoved his hands in his pockets and gave him a flat unfriendly scowl. "What if I do?"

"You knew your father is David Rogerson." Alec's accusation cut through the silence of the snowy night.

"He's not my father."

Matt sounded as if he'd aged a million years and Alec ached to take him back into his arms, but he had to find out the truth.

"The Feds say otherwise."

"Like they always get it right," Matt scoffed.

"Don't lie to me, boy," Alec said harshly. "Is David Rogerson your father?"

MATT

Matt deflated at the anger in Alec's voice. "He fucked my mother and I'm the result. But he's not my father. He wouldn't know the meaning of the word."

He closed his eyes at the pain writ over Alec's face. He'd always dreaded this day and now it had arrived. The truth had come out. He'd had his time with this wonderful man and now it was time to move on.

Alec just stared at him, aged years with one admission. "And you never said anything."

"I tried. I told you when you first dragged me into this that if I got involved, they could kill me." He watched Alec blink, clearly remembering that conversation in the café with Josh Cooper and Quinn Ryder. "But that's not what you're asking, is it?"

"No."

"You're asking why I didn't go to the authorities and tell them what was going on."

Alec swallowed hard. "Yes, I am. You know I have to ask these questions, Matt, because everyone else is going to. The family will want answers."

Matt curled his lip. "You're more worried about what your family thinks than me?"

That cut deep. The idea that Alec put his family first... what was he thinking? Alec always put his family before anything.

"You know that's not true, my sweet boy." Alec stroked Matt's cheek. His fingers were warm against Matt's chilled skin. "But my family deserves answers. You know that."

"Because he told me he'd kill me if I ever breathed a word to anyone. And he showed me how, over and over."

Matt held up his hand. "I'm not gonna tell you the details. Please don't ask me."

Let Alec retain that bit of innocence, even if it cost Matt his Daddy Bear. He didn't need to see the photos. It was bad enough Matt had them playing on a loop in his head.

"Who's *he*?" Alec demanded, his frown deep, clearly unhappy with Matt's response.

"Rogerson."

"Your father said he'd kill you?"

"He's not my father," Matt said harshly. "I told you that already."

He would never call that man his father. He was evil, a monster.

"I'm sorry."

Placatingly, Alec held his hand out, but Matt took a step back. He couldn't let Alec touch him now. He turned, the snow crunching underfoot. He needed to run, to get away, but Alec clamped a meaty hand around his bicep.

"Don't run away from me. Talk to me, please."

Matt refused to meet Alec's eyes, but he heard the pleading in his voice. He couldn't give in. "What's the point? You're not going to believe me."

"Matt, you've never lied to me."

He had to be joking. Their whole relationship had been based on one big lie.

"Talk to me, Matt. Tell me why you're still alive while other boys died." Alec's voice was so gentle, without the anger of moments before.

Matt was so desperate to lay his head on his Daddy's chest and spill out his guts, begging his Daddy to take the pain away. But he would still be the monster in the room because that's the way Rogerson made him.

"He wanted me to live as long as I followed his rules," Matt said dully.

"So you did?"

Matt's laughter was harsh, a sharp contrast to the quiet softness of the snowy glade. "No, I ran away because I'm a coward."

"You're no coward, my boy," Alec declared.

"But I am, aren't I? I ran away from him and left all those boys behind. Lyle and you guys went and rescued them."

Matt found himself pressed against the scratchy wool of Alec's jacket, Alec's large hand cupping his head.

"And so did you. You spent hours and hours with us helping us close the theme parks, helping the boys find new homes, making sure they were safe, and hunting and tracking Greencoats. You were doing your job and working for us. You spent as much time on this as any of us. More really. I spoke to Cooper. He told me about your phone calls. You knew, didn't you, what we were facing?"

Matt sighed. None of them had any idea how big this would be. Except him. He remembered the early days, the sweet brothers' naivety. They were a country family who sold Christmas trees. They had no idea of the evil they faced. He'd tried to dissuade them from getting involved. Told them to leave it to the likes of Cooper and the authorities. But they had to do it, for boys like Lyle and Vinny, and God help him, boys like him. But Matt could tell them what to expect. It was the one thing he could do.

"Aaron once told me my family was too innocent to face the kind of evil your father—Rogerson—perpetrated on the world," Alec murmured above him.

Unseen by Alec, Matt gave a wry smile. He and Aaron talked about this a lot. Aaron had been locked away by his mother until he'd managed to escape when he was only just thirteen. Aaron understood evil in a way the brothers never would.

"I think he was right," Alec continued. "And so were you. We should have left it to the Feds."

Matt leaned back and for the first time locked gazes with him, the blue of his Daddy Bear's eyes dark under the moonlight. "Yet you never stopped."

Alec gave him a rueful smile. "It was too late by then."

"Do you want me to leave now?" Matt was torn between his natural inclination to run and wanting to stay with Alec as long as he could.

Alec's arms tightened around him. "You're not going anywhere."

Matt coughed but Alec didn't let him go.

"You just don't want to upset Vinny," Matt teased.

"And Lyle and Gruff. I really don't want to upset my baby brother...brothers if you include Vinny."

Matt sighed. "It's not going to be pretty, Daddy Bear. Things are gonna come out that I've kept hidden for a long time."

"There's nothing we can't handle together as a family," Alec assured him.

Oh, Daddy Bear, you say that now, but you've got no clue about the monster inside.

"Matt! Matt!"

Matt turned at the sound of his name being called, and Alec let him go. Red and Aaron appeared between the trees. They looked relieved to have found him.

"Come on, it's time we went to the cabin," Red said. "Vinny's gonna have a meltdown if we don't keep up with the plan."

Matt turned back to Alec. "Are we done?"

Alec gave a curt nod. "For now. We'll pick this up after the weekend. Cooper's not bothering us until then."

So he had the weekend to spend with the family before it was all over. He could run now and ruin their celebrations, or he could spend it with them, then deal with the fallout.

Matt licked his lips. "After the weekend?"

"He promised."

Matt turned to Red and Aaron who were watching them curiously. He faked a huge smile. "Come on, then. Let's find the birthday boy and have fun."

Aaron whooped and Red dragged Matt away. Matt looked over his shoulder to see Alec staring after him, his hands in his pockets, snowflakes landing on his hair and beard. Of all the stupid things to go through Matt's head was the thought that Alec was past due for a trim. He was the most particular of the family, always keeping his hair and beard neat, unlike most of the brothers who looked like wild men. A lot of that was down to Matt nagging him to get Brad to clean him up. Would his Daddy Bear remember if Matt wasn't there to nag him?

"Do you want to talk about it?" Aaron said. He and Red stopped and turned to face Matt. "It's us, Matt. You can talk to us. We can find Jack too."

Matt looked at his two friends. "I might not be here for much longer. Not my choice this time," he added to ward off the usual comments about him running away.

Red shoved his hands in his pockets. "What can we do to help?"

"Take care of Alec when I'm gone," Matt said and saw them flinch.

"It's that serious?" Aaron asked.

"Yeah." Matt tried to shrug but it didn't seem to work as

the two men crowded in and hugged him. "He'll need friends."

"He needs you," Red pointed out. "So let's make that happen, brother mine."

Matt blinked back tears. How had he gotten a Daddy Bear and a family, only now to lose them? Life was so fucking unfair.

3

ALEC

All the boys except Lyle appeared from the cabin. They looked happy but exhausted, with deep smudges under their eyes. From the noise coming from the small cabin, the celebrations had gone on long into the night. Each brother had taken a turn to drive up to the cabin, peer in, and report back. When Alec had taken his turn, he saw Aaron snoozing in Matt's arms as the rest played Jenga. Matt had seemed relaxed enough, although he knew his boy was very good at acting.

Alec watched now as Matt glanced around the kitchen, clearly panicking when he didn't immediately see Alec. Ashamed of himself for scaring his boy, Alec stood and waved. Matt weaved in and out of the crowd and Alec held out his arms. Matt stepped into them, and Alec held onto Matt tightly as Lyle was led blindfolded into the kitchen by Gruff. Matt was rigid in his arms, but he had promised not to bolt, and Alec was going to hold him to that promise. He also knew Matt would never want to upset Lyle on his special day however angry he was with Alec.

Jake led the singing and the family joined in. He had a beautiful voice and should have trained as a professional singer, but like all the family, had to give up his dreams to keep the family together.

"I love you," Alec whispered into Matt's ear, knowing no one else would hear it over the family bellowing out 'Happy Birthday'.

Matt sighed and relaxed a fraction. "I love you too, Daddy Bear."

Alec watched as Gruff took off the blindfold and Lyle took in the sight of not just his family, but many of the boys from Kingdom Mountain, singing to him. His eyes went wide, and he turned to Vinny.

"You did this? For me?"

Lyle held out his arms and Vinny rushed into them, and they hugged tightly, sobbing over each other.

Then it was the turn of the Kingdom boys to greet Lyle. They rushed him as Gruff stepped back and Lyle was enfolded in hugs and kisses from boys he'd grown up with. Tears rolled down their faces, however, Vinny was prepared. There were boxes of tissues on the table.

Alec noticed Red and Harry had slipped out. This had to be hard for Red. He'd struggled with the way his life turned upside down after his theme park was shut. Seeing all these boys together had to cut like a knife. He would never get the chance to be with his boys from the water park in Florida. Red didn't talk about it, but Alec was sure there had to be a lingering resentment.

The Brenners stepped back, leaving the boys to greet each other at the tops of their voices.

"I thought this was meant to be a family dinner," Brad muttered at Alec's side.

"That comes later," Matt told him. "Last night was the family boys, now it's the Kingdom boys, and this evening it's the family dinner."

Brad shook his head. "How did you get all the boys here?"

"We organized buses for all the Kingdom boys who wanted to come." Matt grimaced. "Not all of them did. Some boys want to forget about their past. But others love Lyle and wanted to celebrate. Also, it's a party and none of them have had parties in their lives before now. They didn't want to miss out."

"It's a shame about the boys who didn't come," Brad said.

"Vinny sent them all a small gift. No boy is going home empty-handed. You guys need to start saving up, because I cannot tell you how much this weekend cost."

Alec coughed and Matt tilted his head to look at him. "We didn't pay for any of it. Josh Cooper nagged his husband to fund the party. He's a billionaire or something."

Then he wished he hadn't said anything because Matt was back to being rigid in his arms again.

Brad didn't seem to notice as he smiled and watched the boys have fun. They'd peeled off into their age groups and were chatting loudly. Some of them hadn't seen each other since the day Lyle, the Brenners, and the cops and Feds walked into the theme park and changed their lives.

Then Brad turned to him. "How soon can I escape to my barn?"

Vinny turned to face him, his expression fierce. "If you set one foot out of here, Bradley Brenner, I'll tell Lyle to feed you oatmeal for the next month. You're all staying to help me and that's an order."

Alec would have laughed at Brad's horrified expression if he hadn't been dealing with the boy fracturing in his arms.

The party was coming to an end when a slender boy with dark curly hair and olive-toned skin approached them, wearing a cautious smile. He had the deepest brown eyes Alec had ever seen and long thick lashes. He was pretty now but Alec was sure he'd be stunning as he grew older. Alec would put him at about eighteen, a couple of years younger than Lyle and Vinny.

"George?"

"Yes," Matt said warily.

"I'm Eric. I don't suppose you remember me. I helped you in the stables."

"Eric!" Matt's expression cleared. "Of course. I didn't recognize you. You've gotten so tall."

Eric was probably a shade over six feet and built like a reed. "I kept growing," he said ruefully.

Eric wasn't the first to approach them. A few of the older boys, young men really, remembered George, now Matt. They called him both names interchangeably. Some of the boys were almost giddy to meet him again. Alec learned that George had provided a safe haven in the stables when boys needed an escape from the Greencoats. His boy had a huge heart which he did his best to hide.

Eric flicked a glance to Alec, his eyes wide at the size of him. "I...uh...sorry. I didn't mean to interrupt."

Matt smiled briefly. "This is Alec, my boyfriend."

His boyfriend? That knocked the breath out of Alec. It was the first time Matt had ever acknowledged him as his boyfriend outside the family. He wanted to enfold Matt in his arms and kiss him until his toes curled.

Instead, he did the adult thing and held out his hand. "Good to meet you, Eric."

Eric shook, clearly expecting Alec to crush his hand. But Alec, like the rest of the Brenner brothers, never used their strength to hurt people.

"I just wanted to say hello," Eric admitted. "I'm going to art school out of state. It's time I got away from the mountain."

"I kept trying to get away and yet, here I am," Matt said wryly.

Alec barked out a laugh. "Look at me and my brothers. We've never gotten off the mountain."

Brad suddenly appeared at his side. "Hey, Alec. Can you help me get more wood for the stove? It's damn cold today."

Alec's lips twitched. They had suspended the swear jar for today. No one was prepared to cover sixty-plus boys if they cursed.

Eric's eyes grew even wider when he saw Brad. Huge with a bushy beard, Brad looked as if he were grown from the mountain itself. The boy licked his lips nervously. Brad's focus was on Alec, oblivious to the tall, slender man at their side.

Alec held back an eye roll. His brother was always oblivious to men attracted to him. Or perhaps he just wasn't interested. Either way, Eric flagged a little when he realized Brad wasn't going to pay him any attention.

"We'll all help," Matt said.

Brad blinked, seeing Eric for the first time. "I'm sorry, I didn't mean to interrupt."

Alec decided to make introductions before it got painful. "Eric, this is my older brother, Brad. Brad, this is

Eric, he's a Kingdom boy and used to know Matt when he worked in the stables."

Brad and Eric shook hands. Now Alec didn't bother to hide his amusement as they stared at each other.

"Wood?" he reminded Brad.

"Oh, yeah." It took Brad a moment to remember his brother was standing beside him.

"May I help you?" Eric asked somewhat breathlessly.

Without missing a heartbeat, Brad tucked Eric's hand in the crook of his elbow, and they headed to the door.

Matt looked at Alec. "Did I just see what I thought I saw?"

"My older brother gets picked up by a sweet twink? Yeah, you saw it." Alec couldn't hide his smirk. "I don't think he's realized it though."

"It's the first time I've seen Brad interested in a boy."

Alec shrugged. "Brad's always a gentleman but I don't think he's that interested in boys. He's more interested in his explosions and poetry."

Matt looked dubious but he didn't argue the point. "Are we going to help them?"

"I guess we'll have to. Brad will only moan otherwise."

But when they reached the woodpile, they discovered Brad and Eric were...busy.

"I guess the wood can wait," Alec muttered.

Matt chuckled, even if it did have an edge of bitterness. "You know that was all Eric. Brad would never make the first move."

Alec raised an eyebrow. "And how do you know that?"

Matt rolled his eyes. "How long have I known you all, Daddy Bear? None of you were loved up when I first met you. The Brenner Daddies were young, free, and single. I knew all about you guys before I ever met you."

Alec glowered at him. "Oh?"

Matt leaned forward and Alec bent to listen. He whispered, his breath ghosting over Alec's ear, "And I never saw anyone else when I met you. It was only ever my Daddy Bear for me."

Their eyes locked, and Alec saw Matt's Adam's apple bob.

Alec stroked Matt's cheek. "Same, my sweet boy. It was always the same for me."

MATT

Matt fell into Alec's arms and wrapped his around Alec's neck. Behind him, he could hear Brad and Eric kissing, occasionally murmuring to each other, but he didn't care. His whole attention was focused on his Daddy. Alec tasted bitter and sweet, probably from the drinks they'd mainlined. He moaned with pleasure, his desire ramping up as Alec kissed him, soft, drugging kisses that made his dick hard, and him ready to beg his Daddy to spin him around and take him against the wall.

But the cough behind them made Alec raise his head, and Matt moan as he tried to claim back his Daddy's mouth.

"Fuck off," Alec muttered at Harry and Red who didn't bother to hide their amusement.

Harry raised an eyebrow. "I thought you were getting wood."

"They are, Daddy," Red smirked. "Just not the wood you expected."

"We got distracted." Alec nodded in the direction of the woodpile. "Big brother found his entertainment."

Red peered around them, and his eyes widened. "Is that—"

"Yep," Matt said.

"We still need the wood. Vinny's starting to growl."

"What are you all doing here?" Jake asked, holding Aaron's hand.

Alec groaned into Matt's hair.

"Alec and Matt were busy," Harry said. "We're here because Brad and...I've no idea what his name is—"

"Eric," Matt supplied helpfully.

"Brad and Eric got busy by the woodpile, and no one wants to disturb them."

"That's about it," Alec agreed.

"Coming through," PJ boomed. "Vinny's gonna have a meltdown if we don't haul ass back to the kitchen with wood. Brad, fuck your boy in the barn so I can get to the woodpile."

It was effective, if not tactful. Brad scowled at them all, flushing crimson as he realized he had most of his family smirking at him. Then he pulled Eric away and headed to the barn.

"Hurry up," PJ yelled after him. "Dinner is soon."

"You know he's going to kill you," Jack said.

"He loves me." PJ waved his arm, nearly sending Jack flying.

Matt had to admire Jack's reflexes. He probably had to work on those being partnered with a man mountain like PJ. Matt loved the man despite his crassness, but he was a walking disaster at times.

Jack turned on his Daddy. "Geez, PJ, do you want to knock me out again?"

The big man hung his head. "Uh-oh, I'm in trouble."

Jack huffed and stood on tiptoe to kiss his Daddy. "You can make it up to me later."

The others collected the wood while Alec and Matt stayed where they were, Matt leaning against Alec's broad chest, wondering if this was the last time he would feel this safe.

Alec sighed, his breath ruffling Matt's hair. "We ought to go in before Vinny loses the will to live."

Matt chuckled. "I don't think he'll offer to host another party in a hurry. Three parties."

Alec shuddered. "What on earth possessed him?"

"He wanted it to be special for Lyle."

"I don't think Lyle will forget this weekend anytime soon."

When they walked into the kitchen, the Kingdom boys had left, and the kitchen seemed strangely empty.

Matt glanced at Alec. "They left one behind."

Meaning Eric.

"I guess Brad will be taking Eric home." Alec shuffled closer to Matt and murmured, "Uh, how old is he?"

Matt worked it out on his fingers. "I'm twenty-five, Eric is six years younger than me. So he's nineteen."

Alec nodded, looking relieved.

"Checking he's legal?" Matt teased, but Alec didn't return his smile.

"I have to check."

Matt sobered. "I guess you do."

The brothers were obsessed with making sure all the boys were of age. Matt had asked Alec about it, who'd pointed out that certain folk in the town would have loved to make trouble for them and they couldn't rely on the local sheriff to have their backs.

It was then Matt understood why the brothers kept

mostly to themselves except for the occasional visits to the Tin Bar. Seven gay Daddy bears had to freak the vanilla folk out. And no matter what the brothers believed, the town folk were aware of the brothers' proclivities, but most of them minded their own business.

Matt glanced across at Lyle who looked dazed and happy as he sat on Gruff's lap. Gruff pressed a kiss into his palm and his boy leaned into him. Lyle coming into the brothers' lives had turned the family upside down but made them the happiest men too. They had found their boys to make them complete.

He had a feeling Lyle would never forget this birthday. Nor would Matt. He was glad that he'd been given this time to be with his family. *His* family. The only real one he'd had. Rogerson had never been anything more than a sperm donor to a woman who deserved better than him. Matt didn't remember his mom. So his Daddy Bear and all the Brenners were the best family he could ever have.

Then Alec put an arm around him. "Sit down with me? I'd like to cuddle for a while."

Matt leaned into him, whispering, "Can I sit on your lap, Daddy?"

He felt Alec's hitch of breath. He'd never asked to sit on his Daddy's lap, but now he needed it, he needed Alec around him.

"You can always sit in my lap," Alec assured him.

"No sitting, not yet." Vinny shoved plates in Matt's hands. "Lay the table. Alec, you fetch the cups and glasses. Red, make sure there are enough chairs. PJ, if you let that stove go out, you won't like the consequences. Aaron—"

"It's done, it's done," Aaron said hastily, holding up a spoon.

Alec grinned at Matt. "I think we'd better do as we're told before Vinny's head explodes."

"Ha ha," Vinny groused. "You try organizing three parties."

"Hell no."

"Then shut up. Have you—"

Damien took Vinny in his arms and kissed him. It was a toe-curling kind of kiss designed to take Vinny's brain offline for a while and let everyone else sort out the table in peace. When Damien let Vinny go, the table was ready, and everyone waited for fresh orders.

"I included a space for Eric," Matt said.

Vinny frowned. "He should have gone with the others. Where is he? Hell, can we get the coach back?"

"There's no way the coach can turn around anytime soon. Anyway, last time I saw him he was playing tonsil hockey with Brad. I don't think he's going anywhere tonight," Alec said as he flopped down onto his chair and tugged Matt onto his lap. Matt flailed for a second before Alec tucked him exactly where he wanted him.

"Brad and Eric?" Vinny shook his head. "But he's just a baby."

No one laughed. No one said a word. But everyone remembered the determination seventeen-year-old Vinny had put up to claim the eldest Brenner brother.

PJ snorted loudly. It always had to be PJ. "Little bro, you were a baby, and it didn't stop you."

Vinny flushed. "I had to catch my Daddy before someone else did."

Everyone turned to stare at Damien. Of course, his eyes were brimming with tears.

"Sap," Alec muttered, but he sounded choked up too.

Matt shook his head. The Brenners were all huge men

with the softest hearts. Even Jake and Alec, who pretended to be hard-bitten private investigators. Sam Spade, they were not.

Brad and Eric emerged as dinner was served. No one asked what they'd been doing. They both looked as though they'd been dragged through a hedge backward and Eric's shirt was missing a few buttons.

"Big brother looks happy and relaxed," Alec murmured.

"You mean well-fucked," Matt said.

"That's what I said," Alec agreed.

Matt wondered how that would work with Eric going off to art school. But then Alec kissed him, and he stopped worrying about Brad and Eric and concentrated on the only man he cared about.

4

ALEC

It was late into the night before the family left the kitchen. It was only once Lyle fell asleep on Gruff's lap that Matt whispered, "Take me to bed, Daddy Bear."

Alec opened the door to his bedroom and stepped inside. The room was lit only by the soft light of the moon, which filled it with a romantic ambiance. He had to acknowledge that romance had been missing in their lives from the start. Maybe once this business with the Feds was finished, he and Matt could settle down and he could take his boy on dates, and woo him like a gentleman. Matt would like that, even if he wouldn't admit it.

He felt Matt wrap him in a warm embrace from behind and press his cheek between Alec's shoulder blades. Just Matt's touch filled Alec with a peace he'd never felt before. He closed his eyes and lingered in the moment, not wanting it to end.

"I love you, my sweet boy," Alec said softly, his voice barely above a whisper.

"I love you too, Daddy," Matt replied, his voice equally quiet, his hand sliding to rest over Alec's heart.

Unseen, Alec's eyes stung at Matt calling him Daddy.

They stayed in that moment for what felt like an eternity, until Alec turned to shut the door and draw Matt over to the window. He wrapped an arm around Matt's shoulders, and they gazed out, taking in the snowy landscape in silence. There had been a light snowfall during the family dinner, but the temperatures were expected to rise overnight. Alec couldn't even pray for heavy snow to cut them off from the Feds.

"It was a night like this that Gruff found Lyle," Alec said eventually, breaking the quiet.

"If that hadn't happened, I probably wouldn't be here," Matt admitted with a sigh, leaning against Alec's solid chest.

"You always were a love 'em and leave 'em type," Alec agreed.

Matt scoffed. "You guys were just as bad. Remember, I knew you first."

Alec grunted. Matt had a point. They were as bad as each other. But now it was different. Alec prayed that wasn't about to end. He still had so much to give to his boy. He looked down just as Matt tilted his chin to glance up and their eyes locked in a gaze of love and adoration. Alec had never felt so alive and so deeply connected to another person before. He could feel the love and desire radiating from Matt, but also the need to be loved too. He leaned forward and gently kissed Matt's lips, savoring the taste of his full mouth.

"Mmm, hot chocolate."

Matt reached up and kissed him again. "With a hint of chili."

They deepened the kiss, exploring each other and reveling in the passionate intensity of their connection. Alec pressed Matt against him, one hand cupping Matt's head and the other his taut ass. He could feel Matt's arousal, nudging and insistent against his thigh. Matt wrapped his arms around Alec's neck and held on tight as they continued to kiss.

Alec could feel Matt's heart beating against his chest, and it made him feel even more loved. He pulled away from the kiss and looked deep into Matt's eyes. He could feel all the love he had for Matt reflected in his clear gaze, and he knew that this was the moment they had been building up to.

"It's you and me, kid. For the rest of our lives."

Matt's eyes widened. "Is that a proposal?"

"It's a promise. When I think you're ready for a proposal, I'll make one."

"You're that sure of me?"

Matt sounded as if he needed convincing and Alec was happy to oblige.

"I'm that sure of us."

He smiled at Matt and kissed him again, this time more deeply and passionately than before. He felt like he was home, and he never wanted this moment to end.

"Take me to bed, Daddy. Make love to me under the moonlight."

Alec's breath hitched. Just occasionally his feisty brat revealed his romantic heart beneath the spiky exterior. "I'm going to undress you."

He took his time, and Matt stood patiently, as Alec undid the buttons on his shirt, exposing his pale slender form to the adoring moonlight. They were still by the window, drapes open. No one was going to see them and if they did, Alec didn't care if they saw him make love to his beautiful boy.

"I want to see you now," Matt demanded once he was naked.

Alec threw his clothes off without the same care he'd shown Matt's. He heard a chuckle, then Matt pulled Alec closer, his hands roaming over his body, driving Alec wild with desire as he nipped at the base of his throat and rubbed his thumbs over his nipples. Alec reached out to touch him, but Matt moaned, spun him, and pushed him onto the bed. Then clambered on him to gaze down, a wild look in Matt's dark expression.

"I thought I was making love to you," Alec teased, but barely above a whisper. He didn't want to break the mood.

"I want us to make love to each other," Matt murmured.

Alec rolled them so they were facing each other, the moonlight casting a soft glow over their entwined bodies as they explored each other, their passion rising with every touch. He knew Matt as well as his own, yet this was like the first time again. Alec felt like he was in a dream, one that he never wanted to end. They traded lazy kisses, growing more intimate as time went on, yet neither of them seemed anxious to take it to the next stage, pulling back when they needed to breathe, and finding each other's mouths once more.

But inevitably, the needs of their bodies took over. Alec trailed kisses down Matt's chest, sending shivers down his spine. Matt arched his back, offering himself completely to Alec. His shaft nudged Alec's cheek, but aside from one lick around the head, Alec ignored it, moving down to focus on his hip bones. Tonight was about the passion they shared.

When Alec pushed into Matt, the boy groaned and wrapped his arms and legs around Alec. They moved together in a dance of love and passion, their moans filling the room as they pushed inexorably toward their climaxes. Alec felt like he was soaring, his love for Matt taking him higher and higher.

As Alec reached his climax, Matt exploded with pleasure a second later. Alec watched his boy shudder through his orgasm, crying out as their love brought them together in a moment of pure joy. They clung to each other, satiated in a tangle of limbs, their bodies covered in a sheen of sweat and cum.

But Alec was too lazy to clean up. He was ready to drift off to sleep, his boy in his arms. He looked over at Matt, needing to spoon around him. He could tell from Matt's expression that he was deep in thought, but he was smiling and Alec breathed easier.

"What are you thinking about, my sweet boy?"

Matt looked over at Alec and his smile lit up his face. "Just how much I love you, Daddy Bear."

Alec smiled, hiding the momentary sadness at not being called Daddy, and leaned over to kiss Matt. "I love you too." He smiled at Matt, hoping that they would share many more moments like this, moments of loving where their minds and bodies joined together, and the world outside didn't rip them apart.

MATT

When he'd recovered his breath, Matt rolled over and laid his head on Alec's chest. Alec enfolded him in his arms straight away. It was too hot and sweaty, and maybe a little stinky, to be enveloped in a furry bear, but if this was going to be the last time, he would hang onto his Daddy and deal with a little sweat and cum.

That thought constantly rattled through his brain. The last time. The final time. He'd never see Alec again. It was only now it was taken away that he realized how scared he was of the idea. He'd spent the past few years refusing to commit to Alec. At first, Alec had been the same. But their feelings had deepened, and Matt had gone on an endless loop of running and returning, while Alec had always been here on the mountain, waiting for Matt to realize he didn't have to run anymore.

And now he was planning to run again. It was for the best. He kept telling himself that. He knew how to disappear. Matt George would vanish and become someone else, someone with no connection to Kingdom Mountain.

But not yet. Matt promised himself the night with his Daddy.

"Stop thinking," Alec rumbled above him. "I can hear your brain rattling like a hamster in its wheel."

"Nice," Matt grumbled, but he didn't deny it.

Alec carded his fingers through Matt's sweaty hair. "What are you thinking about, sweet boy?"

"How good today was," Matt lied.

"It was fun. Although I don't think Vinny's ever gonna suggest doing that again." Alec gave a wicked chuckle. "I thought his head was gonna explode when that red-haired boy tried to flirt with Damien."

"Vinny was ready to rip his head off," Matt agreed. "You didn't seem to mind when he tried to flirt with you."

"Jealous?"

"No."

That was another lie. Matt had been furious. But Alec had smiled at the kid and dragged Matt to his side and introduced his boyfriend. At that point, any anger seeped away. Alec was his and no strawberry blond twink was gonna have him. The kid had been disappointed to find all the brothers were taken, even Brad, by that point.

Matt felt a momentary sadness that Eric was just a hookup for Brad. He was sweet and it was clear they liked each other. But Eric had plans and they didn't include getting stuck on Kingdom Mountain for the rest of his life. He'd discussed it at the family meal and Brad was vocal in his encouragement, but Matt could see the sadness in his eyes. Like the rest of the brothers, he was hopeless at hiding his feelings. Eric only saw the sweet Daddy urging him to follow his dreams. Matt almost wished he was like Eric, but his Daddy Bear had captured his heart, and leaving for good had never been an option. He always slunk back to his place beside Alec at the kitchen table.

Alec wriggled and stretched underneath him. "I need to have a shower before we sleep."

That was a great idea. At least Matt wouldn't be trying to find somewhere to shower straight away when he left in the morning.

He sat up and looked down at Alec who gave him a lazy, sated smile. Matt's heart cracked a little more.

"Wanna get wet with me?" he suggested.

Like all the bedrooms, Alec's bathroom had a large shower. It was a squeeze with men the size of the Brenners, but Matt had had plenty of practice.

Alec stepped into the shower and drew Matt in with him. Matt groaned in pleasure as Alec shampooed and soaped him, his clever fingers massaging Matt's tired body. He felt the tension of the day slip away as the hot water cascaded over him. He closed his eyes, savoring the moment of intimacy with his Daddy.

Matt reached up and drew Alec down for a kiss, their

soapy, wet bodies pressing together in a wet and slippery embrace. Alec pushed Matt against the tiles.

"Stay there," he ordered.

Sometimes their lovemaking ramped up, and they would tumble out of the shower to land painfully on the tiles, covered in soapy bubbles, arms and legs entwined. Sex in showers meant fresh bruises and Matt didn't care at all while Alec loved on him.

Matt's nails dug futilely into the tiles as Alec's hands roamed over Matt's body, exploring every curve and crevice as his lips followed his fingertips.

He felt himself melting into Alec's touch, the warmth of his body and the firmness of his hands making him feel safe and secure. He knew he was loved, and it made him feel special.

Alec smoothed his hands down Matt's sides as his lips kissed and licked his neck.

"I've got to touch you," Matt pleaded, his hands fluttering above Alec's chest.

He didn't always get permission, his Daddy Bear preferring to take care of him, but this time Alec nodded. Matt's hands were instantly on Alec, smoothing over his chest, feeling the muscles and the strength of his body beneath the fur.

Alec didn't stop loving him for a moment, his hands roaming Matt's body, exploring every inch as they kissed and caressed each other. But soon kisses and touches weren't enough. Matt needed more than that. He whimpered and wiggled and pressed up against his Daddy Bear, trying to show his need.

Alec knew Matt well enough to give him what he desired. He sank to his knees and took Matt's hard shaft down his throat in one fluid movement.

Matt threw his head back and hit the tiles. He saw stars for a moment, but he blinked them away, his whole focus on the huge Daddy in front of him swallowing his dick over and over. Matt's thighs trembled but Alec clamped his hips, not letting Matt move anywhere until he was ready.

"Daddy Bear, please," Matt begged, his fingers carding through Matt's hair. "Please take me back to bed and fuck me."

"That sounds perfect," Alec agreed.

But as Alec got to his feet, he slipped, and Matt lunged for him. They tumbled out of the shower stall onto the floor, Alec shoving one hand behind Matt's head before he smacked it again. Unable to breathe, unable to speak, the air knocked out of him, still covered in bubbles, and with his dick aching for release, Matt sprawled on the tiled floor. Alec was on his side, his gaze fixed on Matt.

"You." Matt coughed, trying to get his lungs to work. "Need to put carpet or cork in here. It hurts, Daddy Bear."

"Whatever you want," Alec promised.

"Whatever I want?"

At Alec's nod, Matt's smile grew wicked to hide his sadness. "I wanna ride your cock."

Alec's eyes widened. "Here? I thought you wanted to go back to bed?"

"I can't wait that long." He scrambled over Alec's thighs. His head ached but he didn't care. All that mattered was the man beneath him.

———

When Matt woke again with a pounding headache, aching everywhere else including his ass, the room was in darkness. He took a moment to orient himself. The party was over, his respite was finished. Now the Feds would want to talk to him.

He rolled his head to look at Alec. He could barely see his features, but he could hear him snuffling and occasionally a light snore.

"Oh, Daddy Bear. Why did you have to find out? I kept it a secret for so long."

He didn't say it out loud, not wanting to disturb him. Matt eased himself out of bed. He'd had a lot of practice running away from Alec in the middle of the night over the years, and he knew how deeply his Daddy slept.

Matt picked up his clothes and bent to brush the lightest of kisses on Alec's mouth.

"So long, my Daddy. I love you. I'm sorry it was never meant to be. I guess our dance couldn't last forever."

Then he dropped a note with three words written on it on his pillow and left the bedroom, hurriedly getting dressed. There was no sound from Gruff's or Brad's bedroom. He'd been worried about meeting one of the other brothers as they all rose early.

Matt had been in the cabin enough times to know which step squeaked and he stepped over it, picked up his jacket and boots, and walked soundlessly to the door, praying that Rexy had slept with Vinny in his cabin and couldn't raise the alarm. Matt loved to snuggle with that dog, but he was a snitch.

But his spot in the kitchen was empty and Matt crept out of the house unchallenged. He was away down the mountain road before anyone stirred.

5

ALEC

The sound of his phone vibrating across the nightstand annoyed the hell out of him. He cracked open one eye. It wasn't light yet. Who the hell was calling him at dark-thirty?

"Go 'way," he slurred when he connected the call. He didn't bother to open his eyes or check who was calling.

"He's on the move," Cooper barked.

Alec sat bolt upright and looked at the space next to him. "Fuck! Fuck! Fuck!" He grabbed the note and scanned the single line. "Fuck! Fuck! Fuck!"

"You could be paying for next year's Thanksgiving by yourself at this rate," Cooper said, not bothering to hide his amusement.

"The tracker's working?"

"Obviously."

"I'm on my way."

Alec jumped out of bed and stood there, unsure of what to do next.

"No," Cooper ordered.

"But—"

"No, we follow the plan. You leave him to us. If you try to interfere the Feds will slap you in cuffs. We need to see where he leads us."

"Matt is my boy."

"And he's our problem, Alec. Take a deep breath. You need to talk to your family first. I promise he won't come to any harm."

Cooper couldn't promise that, but Alec appreciated the sentiment. He exhaled a long breath, hating the thought of not knowing where Matt was. "Call me as soon as he makes contact."

"I will."

Then Cooper was gone leaving Alec, naked in the middle of his bedroom floor, wondering what to do next.

He took a long hot shower, then headed downstairs with Matt's note tucked in the pocket of his flannel shirt. Most of the family sat around the table, looking bleary-eyed, except Harry and Red who usually had breakfast alone. Vinny and Lyle cuddled into their Daddies' laps, while Aaron and Jack sat as close as they could.

Jake fixed Alec with a stare and Alec gave him a brief nod. Then he sent Harry a brief message, receiving an *On our way* immediately. Alec needed coffee. He headed to the machine, then realized he had missed one of his brothers. Where was Brad? He sent a message and his phone buzzed.

> On way up from town. Soon.

"I should start work," PJ said, getting to his feet.

Alec dragged in a shaky breath. "Guys, could you all stay for a while? I need to talk to you."

PJ furrowed his brow, but he sat down, cuddling into Jack.

Gruff waved his phone. "Do you want me to call Harry and Brad?"

"They're on their way. Brad said he'll be longer. He's on his way back from town."

Gruff frowned. "That's early."

"Yeah, he probably took Eric home. He'll be here soon."

Lyle studied him. "Where's Matt?"

"He's gone."

Lyle grunted but didn't ask any more questions. It wasn't the first time he'd given that response. The family were used to Matt's early morning departures.

Alec poured coffee into a large cup and took his place at the table, hoping his brothers wouldn't be long. The quiet intimacy of the four couples was grating on his fragile psyche.

Harry and Red arrived, Brad hard on their heels, and before long they sat around the table, all looking expectantly at Alec, except Jack.

Alec took a deep breath and pulled the note out of his flannel shirt.

"Matt is gone, and he might not come back."

The family's looks of pity were almost more than he could bear, considering what he had to say next.

"He left me a note."

Alec handed it to Lyle. Of everyone here, he deserved to know first.

Lyle read the three words. Gruff looked over his shoulder and cursed loudly.

"Just don't," he said as PJ opened his mouth. "Not until you've all read it."

The note passed around the table, each man blanching and cursing. Vinny read it and burst into tears.

As the last one, Damien read it, placed the sheet of paper on the table, and focused on Alec.

"Did you know?"

"I did." Alec shrugged. "Matt has bad dreams. It took me a while to piece it together, but yes, I knew."

"I'm a Greencoat."

Damien read the words out loud.

"You knew!" Vinny screeched. "You knew he was one of them?"

Damien clamped his arms around his boy, clearly worried he was about to launch himself at Alec. Vinny struggled to free himself, but Damien held on and let Vinny fight through his storm of anger.

Lyle closed his eyes. "I knew too," he admitted quietly and flinched at Vinny's look of betrayal. "I recognized Matt's real name in a list of missing Greencoats."

"So you know the next thing I'm going to say."

Lyle nodded. "I've always known. Matt confided in me when we were younger. I don't know if he even remembers. It wasn't my secret to tell."

"Spit it out," PJ muttered.

"Two days ago, Josh Cooper told Jake and me something we didn't know. Matt's real identity. We always knew Matt George wasn't his real name. He's George Rogerson."

Gruff frowned. "Rogerson? Why do I know that name?"

"Because David Rogerson was the CEO of Kingdom Mountain. He's the man who came here and tried to pretend Lyle had married him. Our Matt, or George is his real name, is his son."

"Son of a bitch," Damien roared.

"Son of a bastard," Jake muttered.

Alec gave him a nod. More accurate.

"So our George who took care of the horses was a Greencoat?" Vinny asked shakily. He seemed to have calmed but Damien still held him close. "That doesn't make sense. He was one of us until he went missing. He was good to me. He stopped them hurting me."

Damien hushed and soothed him, holding Vinny close against his chest.

Alec looked at Jake, begging for his help. Jake nodded and took over.

"We don't have the full story yet. No one does, except Matt. I can't think of him as George. But it seems that Rogerson knew Matt was his son but wasn't prepared to recognize him as such. But as Matt approached eighteen, he had one sliver of humanity in that evil, rotten heart and instead of disappearing his son, he sent him as a Greencoat to another theme park."

"I always wondered how he survived," Lyle said. "I thought he could be like Red, just an anomaly."

"But what happened?" Vinny asked. "You've known him for years."

Alec shrugged. "We don't know. He's been working for Carter and Son as long as I've known him."

"He was on a missing Greencoats list," Lyle said. "The Feds were going to track them all down to see if they could press charges."

"Cooper got ahold of the list and put two and two together." Alec stared down into his cold cup of coffee. "I think that's why Matt could never commit. He knew this would come out one day. And he knew we could reject him." Alec saw Damien and Gruff flinch. It had to be said. They were the ones most likely to turn Matt away.

Vinny knitted his brows. "But George was treated just like us."

"Except he lived," Jake said.

"So did I," Red pointed out.

"You didn't turn into a Greencoat," Harry said, dragging him closer.

"But I wanted to be one." Red licked his lips. "You just stopped it because you closed the place down." The men around the table silenced, all of them staring uncomfortably at Red who shrugged. "All I'm saying is you should listen to him. Not every Greencoat was evil. Most were," he added hastily. "But most of them were one of us at some point."

Lyle nodded. His voice, when he spoke, sounded like crushing dry leaves. "What happens now? Does Matt go in the wind?"

"That's the Feds' problem, not ours," Jake said before Alec could answer.

Alec understood. If they told anyone of the family Matt was being tracked, they could call him out of misguided loyalty and Matt would vanish, never to be in his arms again. He snapped his mouth shut and headed to the coffee pot.

"I don't care what you think. You're all declaring him guilty without talking to him," Jack said suddenly.

Alec turned to see him glaring defiantly around the table.

"Jack—" PJ started, but Jack shook his head.

"Think what you like, but Matt's been nothing but good to me. He's my brother. And you all know he went through the same hell as Lyle and Vinny when he should have been living in luxury as the son of the CEO."

"That's true," Lyle said. "Matt...George...was never treated any differently from us. He was...what...five years older than us?"

Alec nodded. Matt was twenty-five now. There wasn't really a huge gap between him and his boy compared to the others, although sometimes it felt like a lifetime.

"But he slept in the dorms just as we did until he disappeared. Some of the older boys were mean to the younger ones but he never was."

"Why aren't you going after him?" Jack demanded, his attention on Alec. "He's *your* boy."

Knife-like guilt sliced through Alec. But before he could answer, Vinny jumped to his feet.

"But he lied to us. I can't forgive him." He rushed out of the kitchen, leaving behind a stunned silence.

Damien stood with a long sigh, pain in his tired blue eyes. "I'll go talk to him."

Alec knew it was going to be harder on Vinny than anyone else. He'd suffered greatly at the hands of the evil Greencoats. To find out his friend had been one must cut deep and the fact that his best friend and brother knew was a huge betrayal. Lyle looked distraught as he buried himself in Gruff's arms. Alec turned back to the coffee pot. It was going to be a long and painful day.

He jumped as a hand squeezed his shoulder. He turned to see Brad and Jake and then his head was on Brad's broad chest and Jake was rubbing his back.

"It'll be all right," Brad soothed.

"How?" Alec demanded hoarsely. "If the Feds find him, he'll be arrested, and he can't come back here. Vinny will sic Rexy on him."

It was a lame attempt at a joke, but no one was laughing. Brad held him tight, and Jake didn't stop the soothing rub of his back.

"Jack is right. I was wrong. We've always saved our boys," Jake said. "Right from the start. We'll save Matt too."

"We will," Lyle agreed, drawing close to them. "Matt is still one of us. Vinny will calm down, I'll talk to him. You need to go after Matt."

"I don't know where he is," Alec pointed out. He pulled away from Brad as Jake coughed. "What?"

Jake tugged at his beard. "There might just be another tracker on Matt's truck."

Alec stared at him. "You bugged him too?"

"He's family." Jake shrugged like it was a given. "We need to know where he goes. Screw the Feds."

Alec's eyes filled with tears, and he pulled Jake in for a sudden hug. "Thanks, little brother."

Jake thumped his back. "You're welcome. Now let's find him. And no one calls him." He looked around the room at the boys. "We don't want him to vanish."

They all nodded, and Alec prayed they'd obey. If Matt got a call, he'd dump his truck and they'd never find him.

"And the Feds?" Alec asked.

Lyle's smile was almost wicked. "You've got Josh Cooper for that. It's time he did something other than poke his nose in."

MATT

It was sheer dumb luck Matt didn't drive over the side of the mountain road in the dark. His eyes were blurred most of the way down from crying so hard. He wiped them away, but his stupid eyes filled again. He sniffled and cried and sniffled and cried again. He was driving away from the only place he'd called home...the only man he'd ever loved.

"It has to be like this," he said out loud in the confines of the truck. "I have to keep my Daddy safe."

If he stayed, the Feds would come after him. Matt found that thought less scary than his father hunting him down, and in turn Alec. His father...Matt's lip curled...the man didn't deserve the title. The Brenner family and their boys had shown more fatherly love to the kids of Kingdom orphanages than his father ever had. They'd made sure each child was safe, even if like Red, it took a while to get them settled. His father had used and abused children. That was all Matt could say about him.

Tears streaked down his face to drip on his shirt. "I love you, Daddy."

He wiped them away impatiently. He'd been on his own before. He could be on his own again. Meeting Alec and Jake had been a chance encounter at a club, but he'd found himself drawn into their world. It had been fun, going undercover for them and he could flirt with his Daddy Bear and have Alec growl at him. But then he realized they were sucked into *his* world, and it stopped being fun and became a whole lot more dangerous.

Why did Gruff have to find the one boy to blow open the horrors of the Kingdom theme parks?

Matt sniffled again. If Gruff hadn't found Lyle alive under the tree, none of this would have happened. Then he felt guilty because Lyle was one of his best friends and deserved the happiness and love he had now. Lyle had saved so many boys' lives. He deserved a medal, not Matt's anger.

What had Matt done? Run away again, like always. But it was better this way. They could get on with their lives without the monster in their midst. His Daddy and the Brenners thought they knew everything, but really, they'd only skimmed the surface of the depravity of the theme parks. Even Lyle and poor Vinny had been sheltered from the wider picture.

Matt swallowed down the bile that rose in his throat as he thought of some of the things he'd seen.

"It's better this way."

He said it out loud, but it didn't sound any more convincing than when he just thought it.

The Feds would freeze his accounts now he'd gone on the run. The one thing they didn't know was Matt had done this before when he ran from the Greencoats. He wasn't without resources. He had people he could contact for help.

When he got off the mountain and wasn't in imminent danger of killing himself, Matt juggled with his phone and made a call.

"Walker." The scratchy voice sounded like walking over dried leaves.

"It's Tom."

A pause. "Yeah?"

"I need a truck."

"It'll be ready for you after three."

Walker's business didn't ask questions, didn't want real names. Exactly what Matt needed. He would have to save his money, but Walker could help.

He knew where he was going. He had a long drive ahead of him and it would take him most of the day. But first he needed to eat. There was a diner in a couple of miles. He would stop there. The food was good and cheap. He knew the diner well, on his travels to and from the mountain. Then he wondered if he should go somewhere else. If he was gonna hide, he couldn't be so predictable.

Matt turned off the highway and into the large parking lot. He needed predictability one more time. He wasn't surprised to find the diner was three-quarters full, it was always popular.

The waitress greeted him with a cheery, "Matt! I thought you'd forgotten us."

He forced a smile. "How could I forget you, Charlene?"

Her eyes narrowed for a moment as she studied him, then she pointed to a booth and told him she would bring the coffee pot.

"Thanks." His smile was more genuine this time. "Just keep it coming."

He didn't have to order. He'd been here enough; the steak and eggs turned up soon after the coffee.

Matt gave a wry grin at the huge plate. Before he'd gotten involved with Alec, he'd been a small eater like a lot of the Kingdom boys. Starvation did that to you. But the Brenners changed things and now he shoveled food in without a second thought.

The steak and eggs were good and hot, and the coffee plentiful, settling his stomach. He ate the last bite of toast and took a breath for what felt like the first time since Alec had told him he knew about his father.

"More coffee, darl'?"

He looked up and smiled. "Please, Charlene."

She topped off his coffee and left him alone with his thoughts.

Finally he couldn't delay his departure any longer. He needed to get on the road if he was going to get to Wyoming before dark. He paid and left Charlene a healthy tip and a kiss on the cheek.

She surprised him with a sudden hug. "Are you in trouble, Matt?"

"Nothing I can't handle," he lied.

"What about your big ol' bear? Where is he? Why isn't he here?"

He and Alec had stopped by here many times once Matt introduced him to the diner.

"It's better he's not with me."

She fixed him with a piercing gaze. "You're a fool, boy."

The 'boy' made him jump. How did she know?

Because she wasn't stupid. Too many people passed through the diner for her not to be able to read people like a book.

"Maybe," he allowed, "but I gotta keep him safe, Charlene. He needs to be safe."

She grunted, hugged him once more, and turned to serve another customer.

Dismissed, Matt headed out of the door and toward his truck.

"Boy!"

The word was a command. Matt turned to see Alec running at a breakneck speed across the diner parking lot, Gruff and Jake following at a slower pace.

Alec slipped on ice but recovered and hauled Matt into his arms so forcefully Matt would have stumbled if he hadn't crashed into Alec's solid chest. The strong arms around him kept him standing.

"How did you find me?" Matt gasped into Alec's thin sweater.

"You're coming home with me, boy. Don't you dare run out on me like that again."

Matt leaned against Alec, feeling the shuddering breaths under his cheek. "You found me."

"Of course I found you," Alec snapped. "Do you think I'm ever letting you go? You're mine."

He wished that were true. Tears leaked between Matt's tightly closed eyelids. Would he ever quit this damned crying? He clung onto Alec, needing his solid comfort. But Alec was holding him just as hard, seeking the same comfort too.

"We should get out of here," Jake said.

"I'll get his bag," Gruff replied.

Neither Matt nor Alec moved. They stood like that in the middle of the parking lot, not caring what was happening around them. Alec murmured something in his ear and Matt struggled to hear what he was saying.

"You're mine, you're mine. He can't have you!"

On repeat.

"I'm yours." Matt tried to soothe him, but he wasn't sure it penetrated the fear and anger overwhelming Alec. His Daddy was scared. This was his fault.

Misery and guilt swept over Matt, but even in the midst of that, one thing stuck in his mind. His Daddy Bear had come looking for him and Matt wasn't alone.

For now.

6

Seeing his boy hurry out of the diner reassured Alec in a way he couldn't explain.

They'd spotted the truck as soon as they arrived at the diner, but Matt could have just dumped the vehicle and taken off on foot. There was a truck stop not far along. He could have gotten a ride from there.

Jake's face had gotten grim when Alec suggested that. His boy, Aaron, had nearly died when he encountered a trucker who refused to have a f****t in his truck. Even in his thoughts, Alec refused to say the word. That was a double fine in the swear jar.

"We're gonna find him," he promised, "before he gets that far."

Alec hoped so, but when he saw Matt and hauled him into his arms, he breathed easier for the first time since he'd woken up to the phone call saying his boy was on the run.

"You're mine, you're mine. He can't have you," he whispered in Matt's ear.

He wasn't sure whether he was talking about Rogerson or Cooper. At this point they both represented the enemy. He rocked his boy as Matt sighed and pressed into his arms.

"We've gotta move," Jake said.

They climbed into the truck, Jake driving, Gruff claiming shotgun, which left Alec and Matt in the back. Matt had barely settled before Alec hauled him into his arms.

Jake headed back to the highway, and they returned the way they'd come.

Matt looked out of the window. "Are we going home?"

Home. Alec's heart clenched. "Yeah."

"They'll come for me."

"Yeah, I know, but I'll be with you. You don't have to be brave by yourself," Alec assured him.

Matt's laugh was cynical, bitter, it cut like a knife digging into the already gaping wound in Alec's heart.

"I'm not brave, Daddy Bear. If I was, this would never have happened. I would be dead like the others."

Alec swallowed around the lump in his throat. "Don't say that."

Matt turned to look out of the window. "It's true." He sighed. "Who's angrier with me? Vinny or Cooper?"

"At the moment Vinny's probably got the edge," Alec teased. "Who are you more scared of?"

"Vinny. He's damn scary. I can twist Cutie Pie around my little finger."

Alec barked out a laugh and from the front, Gruff and Jake tentatively joined in.

Then Matt sobered. "I've got a lot of making up to do."

"You have, but the family can wait. They'll understand." Alec didn't care if they didn't. He wouldn't let anyone get close to his boy tonight. They would stay in Alec's room and rest. The journey went on and soon they reached the mountain road. Alec glanced out of the window. "The lights are on."

Gruff leaned forward and peered through the dirty glass. "I wonder who switched them on after we left."

"Lyle or Jack," Jake suggested.

Damien would have grumbled about the cost, but he wouldn't have argued. If the family was away, the lights welcomed them home.

"I'm glad," Matt mumbled. He sounded sleepy and it didn't take him long to doze off, slumped against Alec.

Alec's phone vibrated and he fumbled to get it out without disturbing Matt. He looked at the screen.

"Cooper," he announced to his brothers.

"Uh-oh, we're in trouble," Jake sang.

"Thanks for that." Alec didn't need to be reminded they were up to their necks in crap now they'd found Matt.

"Put it on speaker."

"I don't want to disturb Matt." He answered the phone. "Brenner."

"Where are you?" Cooper barked.

"You mean you haven't got me bugged too?" Alec couldn't help the snark.

"You didn't take your own trucks."

Well, that answered that question.

Cooper sighed in his ear. "Brenner, they're gonna find you. You can't go on the run. You were just lucky to get to the diner first."

Alec looked down at the boy sleeping in his arms and gently caressed Matt's hair. He knew their time had run out. As much as he wanted to hide Matt away, he couldn't jeopardize everything they had worked toward for the past two years. Matt wouldn't want that. He'd said as much.

"We're going back to the cabin. Give me twenty-four hours and you can turn up."

"You said that before and he ran," Cooper pointed out.

"He won't run again."

"How do you know?"

"Because I won't let him," Alec assured him, praying to God he could hold that promise.

"You don't get another chance, Brenner," Cooper warned. "If Matt tries to hide, he'll drag you down with him."

"I know. He won't."

He half-listened while Cooper talked to someone in the background.

"You've got 'til tomorrow morning. That's all I can give you."

"I understand."

"And there'll be someone guarding your driveway."

"Okay."

Alec knew plenty of ways to escape from the farm, not using the drive, including a tunnel that led from their property to the old theme park.

"Don't try and be clever, Brenner," Cooper warned.

Alec gaped at the phone before he replied. "How did you...no, don't bother. I don't want to know."

"Best you don't," Cooper said smugly. "Just remember you can't outsmart me. Better men than you have tried."

"Your husband?"

"Never wins. He enjoys the game though."

"This is not a game," Alec said bleakly. "This is my boy's life."

"And I'm as invested as you in keeping him safe. Almost as invested," Cooper amended before Alec could growl. "Ten o'clock." Then he disconnected the call.

"What did he have to say?" Jake demanded.

"We've got 'til ten tomorrow morning and don't even think of letting Matt escape." Alec growled a little because he had to. "They're posting a guard in case we do. They're probably following us now. From the way Cooper spoke, we only just got to Matt first."

"That's more than I expected," Jake admitted.

"That's more than any other Greencoat got," Gruff said.

Alec stiffened and Jake turned on him.

"What the hell, Gruff?"

"Keep your eye on the road," Gruff barked at Jake.

"I could drive this road with my eyes closed," Jake muttered, but he obediently turned back to look out of the windshield.

Gruff huffed then said, "All I'm saying is Matt is getting better treatment than any other Greencoat."

"He helped to rescue all those kids," Alec snapped.

"He did, so he gets leeway to be with you. But don't push it or Cooper will come down on you and he could take us with him."

"Is that what you're worried about? Yourself?"

Alec was genuinely shocked. His youngest brother had always been generous of heart and spirit, wanting the best for everyone.

"Don't be an idiot," Gruff snapped. "I'm worried about Matt, but I'm worried about you too. I know how much you love him and that takes away your perspective. We've just gotten our lives back. Lyle is settled for the first time since I found him. Much as I love Matt, I don't want my boy unsettled or dragged away from his family."

Alec wanted to yell that *his* boy was about to be dragged away from his family, but Gruff's priority was always going to be Lyle. He understood that. It was the way he felt about

Matt. He glanced at his boy, but Matt was still sleeping peacefully, and he wondered how much sleep he'd gotten the previous night.

"I do love him, but I know this must be done and so does he."

"Then why did he run?" Gruff asked quietly, the heat seeming to have died away.

"Because I wanted everyone to be safe," Matt said sleepily, raising his head to look at Gruff. "Things are settling down. You don't need my shit on top of everyone else's."

Gruff turned to look at Matt and rolled his eyes. "Matt, do you know Alec at all? Do you know us, the Brenners? Did you not think for one second the family would mobilize? We're the Brenner brothers. It's what we do."

Matt huffed out a laugh. "I guess I wasn't thinking straight."

"You certainly weren't," Alec muttered with feeling.

"You'll be lucky if he doesn't tan your ass," Jake added.

"I can handle my own boy, thanks," Alec said.

He didn't need the pointed silence from the front. His brothers were too damned cheeky.

When they reached the cabin, Jake parked up. Lyle came out to join them. He gave Matt a fierce hug and kissed his cheek.

"Damien and Vinny are spending the rest of the day in their cabin. They don't want to be disturbed."

Alec pressed his lips together, but Matt touched his arm.

"It's all right, Daddy Bear, Vinny needs time to calm down."

He nodded, not wanting to upset Matt any further. Lyle

smiled at them gratefully and Alec realized he'd been
expecting fireworks.

"The rest of the family is working. We'll meet for dinner
tonight. I've left you sandwiches."

Matt grimaced. "I don't think I can eat anymore."

"All the more for us," Jake said cheerfully, walking past
them into the cabin.

Gruff tugged Lyle into his arms. "Let's have some us
time, sweet boy."

They went back into the cabin, which left Alec and Matt
alone on the stoop.

Alec held out his hand. "I think you and me time sounds
just right."

Knowing he had little time left with his boy made him
feel sick and from Matt's expression, he felt the same way.

"I agree," Matt said shakily, taking Alec's hand. "Take
me to your bed?"

If only Alec could handcuff his boy and keep him there
forever.

MATT

Matt stood in the bedroom, not sure what to do. Alec had
been caught by Jake in the kitchen and it had been clear by
Jake's uncomfortable expression, he wanted to talk to Alec
alone. Alec had sent Matt up to the bedroom.

The area around the bed was a disaster zone. Alec had
clearly rolled out of bed and hit the ground running,
judging by the mess of bedclothes on the floor.

If only Alec would bind him in ropes so he couldn't get
away, and Matt would stay there forever, loved by his beautiful Daddy Bear. Once he'd cleared up the mess.

Alec stepped up behind Matt and wrapped his arms

around him. "Sorry, I'll make the bed. I was in a hurry this morning." He added a growl to his voice which made Matt shiver.

"Let me tidy up," Matt begged, wanting to do something, however small, to take care of his Daddy.

"We'll do it together," Alec said, but he held onto Matt for a while longer, and his sigh, when he stepped back, clutched at Matt's heart.

It didn't take long to pick up the items from the floor and remake the bed. Alec took the dirty sock from Matt's hand, threw it in the direction of the hamper, and walked him back to the bed.

"You missed," Matt pointed out.

"I don't care."

Matt felt the mattress hit the back of his legs and Alec kept going, pushing Matt onto the bed, and falling on top of him in a messy tangle of limbs. It was impossible to move, Alec's body pushing him down, his mouth claiming Matt's.

Matt couldn't even loosen his arms to wrap them around Alec's neck, but he realized that's what Alec wanted, total control of him. He'd scared Alec by running away and now the authorities were going to take him away and Alec had no control over that. The only thing he could control was this moment right now. Matt was his and no one else's. And Matt wanted to submit to his Daddy. He didn't want to be nurtured. He wanted to be fucked.

He made a noise in the back of his throat and Alec growled. Outright growled. And claimed his mouth harder. Matt parted his lips and Alec pushed his tongue inside for their tongues to dance a lazy duet.

Alec raised his head. "You taste so good."

"Steak, eggs, and coffee," Matt said, a smile curving his

lips, looking up into his warm blue eyes. He'd hold onto those beautiful eyes of his Daddy for the dark days to come.

"My favorite taste."

Alec bent to kiss him again, a long lingering kiss that made Matt's toes curl and his body arch up to shamelessly press his hardening cock against Alec.

"Patience, my boy. Patience."

Now it was Matt's turn to snarl, but when Alec just raised an eyebrow, he subsided with a pout.

Alec bent forward and nibbled his bottom lip. "I want you as much as you want me. I'm gonna bury this thick cock inside you soon enough, sweet boy." And he rocked his hips against Matt who wanted to crow in triumph. Oh yeah, his Daddy wanted him bad.

He sank into Alec's kiss again, the feel of their tongues sliding against each other sending hot sparks to his dick.

Then Alec pulled back with a sigh. "I want to feel you against me."

They had been entwined but Matt knew what he meant, skin against skin, bare naked cocks sliding against each other.

"I want that too," he agreed.

Alec pulled Matt up and undressed him slowly, pressing hot, wet kisses to each new piece of skin he exposed. Finally, he pushed Matt's jeans down and knelt at his feet, Matt holding onto Alec's shoulder as Alec tugged them off his feet. It was complicated. They'd forgotten to remove his boots first. Matt didn't care. Alec's hands and mouth were all over him, loving him, making him his. Alec even pressed a kiss on the top of his feet. Matt squirmed a little. Alec's beard and mustache tickled his skin, but damn it was hot.

"I want to undress you," Matt begged as Alec tugged off his sweater.

Alec nodded and Matt pulled off his undershirt, dropping it to run his hands over Alec's fur-covered chest.

"We just tidied this up," Alec chided gently, but Matt knew he was teasing. Matt was the tidy one, Alec couldn't care less.

"Don't care," Matt growled. "Need my Daddy Bear." He pinched Alec's copper nipples, dragging a gasp out of him.

"Take my pants off," Alec ordered.

Matt knelt and removed his boots, undid the fastening of his jeans, and tugged both them and his briefs down Alec's thick, muscled thighs. He tugged them off, then placed his hands on Alec's furry thighs and licked down the length of his cock, eliciting a groan from Alec. He tugged on Matt's hair.

"I love seeing your mouth around my dick, sweet boy, but that's not what I want now. It'll be over too quickly. I'm so close to the edge."

Matt eased himself to his feet. "What do you want?" he murmured, gasping as Alec picked him up and tossed him on the bed.

"I want you to roll over onto your hands and knees and show me your sweet hole because I'm going to bury myself in there."

Matt did as he was ordered, his ass presenting to his Daddy as he had many times before, his forehead brushing the sheet.

"So hot," Alec moaned, his warm breath ghosting over Matt's ass cheeks and hole.

It *was* so fucking hot. Matt felt as if he was gonna crawl out of his skin if his Daddy didn't hurry.

"Please, please," Matt begged, although he wasn't sure what he was begging Alec for. Maybe a Daddy's touch, maybe his thick cock buried inside his boy. Whatever it was, it had to happen soon before Matt's untouched cock spurted over the sheets.

He yelled loudly at the feel of Alec's tongue at his hole. Oh God, Alec knew that rimming Matt reduced him to a boneless heap. *Bastard!* But he didn't say it out loud, because one, the swear jar, and two, there was a risk Alec might stop to punish him and he really didn't want that to happen. Matt rested his head on his fists, his focus narrowed down to the tongue licking around his hole, licking and licking, then pushing in, and licking around the muscle again. Matt whimpered, trying to push back.

"Hold still, boy," Alec ordered, his fingers digging hard into Matt's hips.

Matt drew in a shaky breath. His Daddy was always in control and Matt just had to take and take. He screwed his eyes up tight and felt Alec push in with his tongue again, stabbing over and over until Matt needed to wriggle and writhe.

"I can't last much longer," Matt confessed.

His climax coiled like a snake at the base of his spine ready to explode out of his balls. Fuck, that was weird, but he didn't care. He just needed to come, he really needed to come.

Then he cried in frustration as Alec pulled away. "Daddy, please."

Alec's chuckle was low and wicked. "You wait, my boy."

"I hate you," Matt grumbled and yelped as Alec popped him on the butt.

Alec leaned over him. "You want me to stop?"

"No, please don't stop," Matt begged. "Please don't stop."

"What do you want, boy?"

Matt heard the *snick* of the lube bottle.

"All I want is my Daddy's dick inside me," Matt confessed, wriggling his butt to emphasize just how much he really needed it. Alec was a man who needed words and loved it when Matt vocalized his need. Matt had been in a relationship where he was supposed to keep silent and take it. His Daddy Bear wasn't like that. He wanted to hear it all, loving Matt spill out his pleasure and frustration when Alec didn't get the fuck on with it.

Two fingers slid inside him.

"Tell me what you want, boy."

"I want my Daddy's cock inside me."

"You going to be good?"

"Yes, Daddy, I'll be good."

Matt's hole was stretched, widened, and filled as Alec pushed his thick cock inside.

"Oh God, Daddy, that feels so good."

Alec thrust slow, long, and deep. "I know it does," he said softly. "I know."

Matt moaned as he felt his balls being squeezed, his orgasm building until his cock pulsed with the need to come.

"Daddy, please... Please let me come."

"Not yet." Alec's voice was still soft.

"I need to come," Matt begged, his hole clenching tight around Alec's cock when he tried to pull out, the need to be filled again was so strong.

"No, you don't." Alec held still.

Matt started to panic. "Daddy, please... Please... Please..."

"I'm not going to stop, boy."

"Then let me come."

"Not yet."

Matt's body was shaking. He was almost sobbing. He was so close to coming. Alec knew it. Matt knew it.

Matt cried out when Alec pushed back in, his cock sliding deep before pulling out, then pushing in again.

"You want to come, boy?" Alec demanded, thrusting hard so his balls thudded against Matt's ass.

Matt felt as if he was going to come apart. He was shaking and he couldn't keep his ass still.

"Please," Matt begged. "Please..."

"Say it."

"I need to come."

"Do you?" Alec thrust hard.

"Yes, I need to come."

"Then come for me, boy."

Matt closed his eyes, his face scrunching up as his orgasm hit, strong and hard.

"That's my boy," Alec said, his voice full of pride.

Matt was barely aware of his Daddy's hand wrapping around his cock and pumping his orgasm out of him, his body bucking and jerking.

"You're mine," Alec said, his thrusts short and hard as he shot into Matt's clenching hole. "You'll always be mine."

Matt prayed that was true. He really prayed that was true.

7

ALEC

lec held Matt close and insisted they nap for a while, but he was woken by his growling stomach and realized he hadn't eaten all day. Matt had eaten steak and eggs, but Alec had survived on coffee and fumes and worry. He tried to ignore the hunger pangs, but it was as if a bear was trying to crawl out of his stomach. He was surprised the rumbles hadn't woken Matt, but the boy had passed out in his arms the second Alec told him to sleep. His boy was good at obeying orders. Some orders, at least.

He gently disentangled himself from Matt and headed into the bathroom. He avoided looking at himself in the mirror, knowing what he'd see, a frightened Daddy Bear, desperate to run with his boy and never be found.

When he returned to the bedroom, Matt had rolled over onto his back, his wrists crossed over his head, his chest and flat belly exposed, pale skin with a dusting of body hair Alec kept threatening to shave and never did, with the covers tangled around his hips, his soft dick just peeping over.

Alec wanted to crawl back into bed and take his boy again, but he really needed to quell the beast in his belly. He shrugged on a robe and crept quietly out of the bedroom.

The kitchen was empty except for Vinny, a lone figure who sat at the table, peeling potatoes. Alec furrowed his brow. Lyle had said Damien and Vinny were spending the day together in their cabin, so what was Vinny doing here alone and clearly miserable from his expression?

"Vinny?" Alec spoke quietly, not wanting to make him jump. "Is everything okay? You haven't fought with Damien?"

Vinny sighed and looked up. "No, we're fine. Damien's in the office and I needed time to think. Are you hungry? Lyle left food in the fridge."

He went to get up, but Alec waved him back down. "I can sort it. You stay there. Hot chocolate?"

Alec needed something to ease his rumbling belly and the pan of hot chocolate was already on the stove. Vinny nodded and murmured his thanks when Alec put a mug in front of him. Alec focused on putting a tray of food together for him and Matt. He didn't want to eat in the kitchen away from his boy when their time together could be measured in hours.

"Alec?"

He turned at Vinny's strained voice. "Yeah?"

"Do you hate me?"

Alec blinked at the question. "Hate you? Why would I hate you?"

Vinny hung his head. "Because I'm angry at Matt."

He sighed and walked over to Vinny, kneeling beside him. He didn't touch him. They were alone and that wasn't his right. But he looked at him, his expression serious.

"No, I don't hate you and neither does Matt. We know you're hurt and upset."

"Matt could have stopped it."

Alec knew what Vinny meant. He could have stopped the Greencoats hurting Vinny.

"And they would have killed him."

"So he says."

Alec sighed. "My boy isn't a liar, Vinny. He did what he had to do to keep living and not be disappeared. I know you don't believe him, but I do."

"He's your boy," Vinny shot back. "Of course, *you* believe him."

"Are you angry at Matt or angry at me?" Alec asked.

Vinny looked down at the half-peeled potato in his hands, "I'm angry at all of you," he finally admitted. "You all believe Matt."

"And you feel betrayed?"

The boy nodded. Alec took a chance and gathered Vinny's small hand in his. "Matt is my boy whether he wants to admit it or not. And I would walk through fire for him, as Damien would for you. I know things you don't, things he's told no one, not even me. He talks a lot in his sleep." He sighed and squeezed Vinny's hand. "But I love you too, little brother. And you have a right to be furious at Matt. He kept his past from you. But my boy is going to be taken away by the Feds tomorrow and I need to share my hours with him because I don't know when...if...I'll see him again."

"Damien said Matt could be the key to bringing them down."

Alec stood, needing to stretch out his muscles. "I think

Lyle did that already, and you and all the other boys. Matt is just one more nail in their coffin."

"He was a Greencoat," Vinny said, his voice harsh.

And that was the crux of the problem for Vinny. Alec knew that. The Greencoats had tortured Vinny. If Matt had been a Greencoat, wasn't he evil?

"He escaped because he couldn't stand to become like the Greencoats," Alec explained. "Rogerson wanted to keep his son where he could control him. Matt wanted to escape."

"What if they lock him up with the others?"

"It's one outcome," Alec admitted. Jake had warned him of this. It would kill him, but he had to face the truth. Matt was as much on the side of the devil as he was the angels, simply by his history. "I'm going back to Matt."

"I love him too," Vinny admitted so quietly Alec barely heard him.

"He knows you do," Alec said. "And he understands why you feel betrayed. He loves you too."

He left Vinny alone with his thoughts as he took the tray upstairs.

In the bedroom, he found Matt sitting up looking sleepy and disoriented.

"You're awake," Alec said. "Are you hungry?"

Matt yawned, then said, "Where were you?"

"I needed food," Alec said, putting the tray on the nightstand so he could cuddle his boy.

Matt sighed and snuggled into his arms. "You were a long time."

Alec hesitated, then he said, "Vinny wanted to talk."

"Is he still angry with me?"

"Yes," Alec admitted.

"He has a right to be. I know I would be in his shoes."

"He still loves you but he's very young. It's gonna take him a while to unravel his feelings. Give him time."

Matt snorted. "It's the one thing I don't have, Daddy Bear." At Alec's flinch, he reached him and cupped his jaw. "I'm sorry, I didn't mean to hurt you."

Alec hugged Matt hard, drawing a squeak from him. "I don't want to think about it for now. It's just you and me in here."

He let Matt go and reached over for a travel cup. "Drink and eat. Lyle left us sandwiches and chips and soup."

Matt gave a wan chuckle. "He's never going to let us go hungry, is he?"

Alec raised an eyebrow. "This is Lyle we're talking about."

"I hope you've got other plans for us apart from eating," Matt said with an attempt at his usual flirtatiousness.

"I have plans," Alec assured him and let the air between them grow thick and heavy.

"Oh yeah?" Matt's voice grew husky. "Like what?"

"Eat up and you'll find out."

Matt pouted at him. But an hour later, when he lay on his back, gripping the headboard, his legs over Alec's shoulders as Alec stared into his eyes and slowly ground into him, over and over, beads of sweat breaking out across Matt's forehead and down his sternum, he wasn't pouting as Alec told him he loved him, he would always love him, and there would be no other boy for Alec, whatever happened.

"You promise?" Matt gasped as Alec pushed in again.

"You have my word," Alec growled. "You come back to me, do you hear?"

"I promise," Matt said, his eyes fixed on Alec's.

Alec was determined these were promises they could both keep.

MATT

Matt awoke feeling as if he were slowly cooking down his back. It didn't take too many brain cells for him to realize Alec was holding him so tightly he couldn't move. His Daddy had held him like that all night. Usually, they fell asleep wrapped around each other and slowly drifted apart to their own sides of the bed overnight.

Not this time. Alec refused to let him go under any circumstances. Even when Matt protested that he needed to breathe, Alec had told him to get over it. Matt understood. It was their final night together and Alec wouldn't let him out of his grip.

The previous evening had been a mixture of sex and food and cuddles and sex and food. By the time they'd stumbled upstairs to sleep for what was left of the night Matt's ass was sore from being pounded through the mattress, his heart ached from the misery the family, minus Damien and Vinny, was trying to hide, and he was sure he'd have a bruised hand from how hard Alec held it.

Matt tried to wiggle around so he could look into Alec's blue eyes, but Alec just grumbled and held him tighter.

"I want to kiss you," Matt tried.

The grip lessened a fraction and he managed to achieve his objective and face him, but Alec's eyes were still closed, and he tangled their legs together and still held onto Matt. Matt guessed he could have broken free, but he didn't want to.

He studied Alec's face, noting the fan of lines etched deeper around his eyes and the grooves in his cheeks. He looked tense already and they'd only just woken up. Single gray hairs shot through his chestnut beard and mustache. He was thirty-four and still beautiful, but he looked older now. Stress had added years to his face. Matt knew he was responsible for some of those lines. He smoothed along one with his fingertip, and Alec groaned, a rumbling, happy sound.

"I love you, Daddy Bear," he murmured.

Alec reared up and pushed Matt back against the pillows. "I love you with all my heart. You will always be my boy. Whatever happens, that won't change. I'm going to make the Feds' life a misery until they return you to my arms."

Matt blinked away the sudden tears. "I don't know what being a boy is about. We never had time to explore beyond playing at it."

"We will do," Alec promised. "When you come back to me, we're going to explore your needs."

It had never occurred to Matt how much he wanted that opportunity, a chance to find out who he really was. He'd floated through life, determined to escape his childhood, and now he was being dragged back to the nightmare. Would he ever get a chance to truly be a boy and not just play at it?

"What's the time?" he asked.

Alec leaned over him and fumbled for his phone. "It's seven-thirty. We've got to be downstairs by eight-thirty for breakfast. Lyle's orders."

"I have to go to my doom with a full stomach."

He meant to sound teasing, but he obviously missed the mark because Alec said, "Let my family take care of you, yeah? They need this."

"Do you think Vinny will be there?"

"I don't know," Alec admitted. "He was real upset last night."

"It doesn't matter." Matt sighed. "It's nice of Lyle to take care of me."

Alec nodded. "And now I'm going to take care of you."

He slithered down the bed, pushing the covers down with him. Matt shivered for a moment with the sudden chill, then Alec nestled between his legs and Matt forgot about the cold and everything else except his Daddy.

Matt groaned loudly as Alec licked his cock from root to tip, licking around the glans, dipping into the slit. He wasn't fully hard, not yet, but with the attention it wouldn't take long. He closed his eyes, then opened them again. He didn't want to miss a second of his Daddy pleasuring him. He watched his glistening cock slide in and out of Alec's mouth.

"I love you, Daddy Bear," he murmured.

He relaxed against the pillows and let his Daddy pleasure him, because they both needed this connection. When would they have it again?

———

Damien and Vinny weren't at the breakfast table, and neither was Rexy. That was a shame. Matt would have liked to say goodbye to the little dog. Everyone else was, and they all gave him a hug as Matt entered the kitchen. They were a little late, because they both had desperately needed that shower, which turned into another excuse to grope each other.

Lyle gave them the side-eye and looked pointedly at the clock. "I was about to send Gruff up to find you."

"Sorry," Alec apologized. "We were busy."

Busy, the family euphemism for getting fucked through the mattress. Matt hid his smile. They'd all used it.

Lyle grunted and to appease him, Matt hurried over to help him serve the breakfast. He gaped at the amount of food.

"How many people are you feeding?"

"I needed to think, and you know cooking helps."

Matt hugged him, an arm around his shoulder. "Will you make sure my Daddy eats properly?"

Lyle turned to hug him with both arms. "I'll teach him to cook until you return, then he can feed you."

They both laughed even if it was shaky. Matt's cooking skills at the theme park had been notoriously bad. It was a good thing he was so amazing with the horses.

Breakfast was loud and boisterous, everyone trying to prove everything was normal, even though it so clearly wasn't. Alec had dragged Matt onto his lap and fed him. It wasn't something they normally did, it wasn't something Matt really liked, but Alec needed it and he would give him anything for their last few minutes.

The knock at the kitchen door as they finished breakfast wasn't a surprise. Matt burrowed into Alec's arms as Lyle answered the door.

"Mr. Cooper," he said coolly.

Cooper was there flanked by two men in trench coats, one of them a stunning silver fox. Matt would have been all over him before he met his Daddy.

"I'm sorry, Lyle, but Matt needs to come with us."

"He hasn't done anything wrong," Lyle said. "He was one of us."

Matt gave him a wan smile. "It's all right, Lyle. We knew this day would come, especially once you stuck trackers on my car."

Lyle tried to force a smile but without much success. Gruff tugged his boy into his arms and whispered something in his ear. Lyle nodded and disappeared out of the door.

The silver fox in the trench coat came over to them. "Mr. Rogerson needs to come with us now."

"My name is Matt George," Matt said. He was never going to use his father's name. It had never been his.

"Mr. George," the Fed agreed.

Matt hung on as Alec wrapped his arms around him.

"You can question him here," Alec barked.

"I'm afraid that's non-negotiable," Cooper said, his expression one of regret, but firm. "Matt needs to be questioned with the other Greencoats."

"No!" Alec was holding Matt so tightly he could barely breathe.

Matt tried to get Alec to focus on him, but his attention was on the Fed. "Daddy Bear, please. It's all right. I have to be questioned."

Part of him wanted to point out Alec was the one who had arranged this. Matt had tried to flee. But he knew Alec wasn't thinking clearly.

"Then you'll return him to me?" Alec demanded.

"We'll keep you informed," Cooper said.

Matt noticed the scowl the silver fox shot the younger man. Cooper was interfering where he wasn't wanted. But if Matt had to leave, at least Cooper had his back.

Alec refused to let Matt go. "I'm coming with him."

The Fed shook his head. "That's not possible, Mr. Brenner." He turned to Cooper. "We have to leave if we're going to meet our flight."

"I'll take care of your boy," Cooper said. "He'll be safe."

Alec dragged Matt tighter against him. "You'll come

back to me. I'll be here waiting for you. The lights will be on until you're returned to me." His voice was thick and choked up.

Matt pulled away because Alec was never going to let him go. "I'm ready," he said to the Fed. He didn't even know the guy's name. He guessed it wasn't important to know who was about to destroy your life.

At least they didn't handcuff him as they led him to a black, nondescript sedan.

He turned to look out of the back window to see Alec in Damien's arms, clearly sobbing, and his brothers surrounding him, patting his back. At least his Daddy wouldn't be alone. Even Vinny was there, Lyle holding him close.

Matt turned to face the front, eyes bleak. The lights around the tree at the driveway were on and Matt knew Alec wouldn't turn them off. It was the only comfort he could take into the unknown future.

"I'll get you home," Cooper said, patting Matt's thigh.

"Can you make that promise?" Matt demanded.

The silence was answer enough.

8

ALEC

The day started with a phone call Alec had waited to receive for six months.

"He's on his way," Cooper said.

He'd begun to think it would never happen as the Feds had held Matt month after month. No trial, no sentence. Just refusing to release him until they were good and ready. It nearly killed Alec.

He sent out the message to the whole family, then threw his phone on the bed and wept into his hands. Being tugged against a large chest a few minutes later didn't surprise him.

"You've got to clear up this pit," Brad murmured as he rocked him. "It stinks."

Alec sniffled and laughed and cried some more.

Several hours later, he opened the kitchen door at the

loud knock. Matt stood there, flanked by the same two men who'd taken him away. He was rail thin. Alec's heart clenched at the sight of his boy. Matt looked haggard, his eyes sunken depths in his pale face and he badly needed a shave. His beard was scraggly. Alec did not approve, and he was sure that was the oversize flannel shirt he'd been wearing when the Feds took him away. It had been one of Alec's old shirts.

Matt gave him a wan smile. "I saw the lights, Daddy Bear."

"They've never turned off, not even for a second," Alec said. He opened his arms and Matt fell into them, sobbing. Alec held him tight to his chest, refusing to let him go, even for a second.

Behind him, the silver fox looked at Alec. "He's all yours."

"You won't take him again?" he queried, wanting to make sure he understood.

The younger man, maybe early thirties, shook his head. "Mr. George has told us everything we need to know. He's free to go."

Alec took a moment to process that, then he ignored everyone as he swept Matt off his feet and clutched him to his chest. Matt buried his face in the curve of Alec's neck, tears slaking his skin.

"The rest of you can greet him later. For now he's mine."

He couldn't bear to put Matt down for a second. He caught the eyeroll from Jake and Vinny's tight expression. Yeah, Matt was going to have to repair a few bridges, but it would happen in time. Alec had faith in his family. Later.

Behind him, Alec heard Lyle talking to the Feds, but he didn't care. The only thing that mattered to him was Matt in his arms. He walked up the stairs to his room, paused at the threshold, and looked into Matt's swimming eyes. "You're never leaving again. Do you understand that? You sleep in my bed, in my arms, because that's where your Daddy orders you to sleep."

Matt nodded and more tears spilled onto his cheeks. "I'm staying like this forever."

Alec grunted. "Good." He would make it clear again and again if he had to. His patience had officially snapped.

He kicked open the door and dropped Matt onto the unmade bed and straddled his thighs to press him down. He didn't care about the wreck of the covers. He just needed Matt where he should be.

Matt placed his hand over Alec's heart. "I can hear your heart beating." He sounded almost awed.

He fixed Matt with a stern glare. "It's beating for you, boy. Just for you."

Matt's fingers spread out over his chest. "I never thought I'd get the chance to do this again. I thought..." He met Alec's eyes. "I didn't think you'd want me back. It's been so long with no contact."

Alec raised an eyebrow. "The Feds didn't tell you I've been calling them every day? They wouldn't let me visit you."

"They did on the way up. They said they never wanted to speak to you again." Matt sounded smug about that.

Alec couldn't help the lip twitch. He had been damned annoying, and he didn't regret a second of it.

Matt cupped Alec's cheek. "They told me you were a fucking pain in the ass, but when it came to let me go, there was only one place to bring me."

"I would have collected you," Alec assured him. "All you had to do was call."

"The Feds wouldn't let me call you. No one was supposed to know where I was." Matt caught Alec's expression. "Cutie Pie told you?"

Alec made a disgusted face. "Yeah. He called this morning. Of course he knew. The little weasel knows everything. But he knows everything about everyone."

"Where is he now?"

"As soon as he knew you were being released, he went home. His husband was ready to tear him limb from limb if he didn't return to London."

"He was good to me."

Cooper was, but Alec was done talking about him or anyone else. All he wanted to do was bury himself in Matt's body and reclaim him.

Matt must have recognized the pain in Alec's expression because he said, "Make me yours again, my Daddy."

Alec sucked in a deep breath. Matt had so rarely called him Daddy. Only in their quiet moments together. "We need to talk."

"Now?"

Alec grinned at the full-on whine from his boy. "Now."

"I thought you wanted..."

"I do, boy. But we need to talk first." He brushed Matt's lips with his, hiding his grimace at the bitter taste of cheap coffee and stale breath. His boy needed a shower, but it could wait. Alec would bathe him in Damien's big tub.

He sat up and pulled Matt with him into his arms. Matt huffed but settled against his chest. For the first time in six months, Alec felt he could relax. His world was right again, and Matt was where he should be.

"What I want is to take you in my arms and fuck you until neither of us remembers our own name."

"I want that too," Matt agreed. He snuggled in closer and yawned and Alec stroked down his back.

"But..."

Matt stiffened in his arms. "But?"

"But I need to know I'm what you really want. Forever. I can't go on like we were, Matty. You were mine and then not, mine and not. It was endless. I need you to be mine forever. Live with me in my arms and my bed. Work for me and Jake. Find your place in our house. Or..."

Matt raised his head and Alec could see the fear in his expression. "Or?"

"Walk away. Give both of us a chance to start again."

"Is that what you want?" Matt asked, scared he was going to be told to leave his Daddy's arms.

"You know it's not. I've just told you what I want. All I've ever wanted is for you to stay right here."

"I was scared," Matt admitted. "What would you do if you found out my secret?"

"And now you know. I'd love you forever, just like I've always done. But my patience is finished, little one. You have to make a decision."

Matt shuddered in his arms. "It's so scary."

Alec held him tighter, wishing he could take the fear away from Matt's heart. "Making a decision?"

Matt shook his head. "I've always known I wanted to stay with you. From the moment we met in that club and you offered me a job."

"I wanted to offer you a spanked butt," Alec admitted. "You were so cheeky."

"You *did* spank my butt," Matt said. "I couldn't sit down for a week."

Above Matt's head, Alec gave a smug grin. He'd been

determined the cheeky boy would never forget his Daddy Bear. Then his grin faded. "Then why is it scary, my boy?"

"What happens if you decide you don't want me anymore? Where will I go? If I give my life to you, I'll have nothing if it goes wrong."

Alec pressed a kiss to the top of Matt's head. "It's not gonna happen, but if it does," he said before Matt could protest, "you'll have what all our boys have. Your own bank account with enough money to start again somewhere. None of us would leave our boys with nothing."

Matt grunted. Alec wasn't sure if he believed him or not.

"Besides, you already have more than enough money salted away."

Matt raised his head, his eyes comically wide. "How the hell did you know that? Did Cooper tell you?"

Alec rolled his eyes. "Oh please, what kind of investigator would I be if I didn't check my boy could cope if something happened to us?"

Matt buried his head back against Alec. "I can never keep a secret from you."

It wasn't true but Alec understood what he meant.

"Just you remember that." Alec sighed and stroked Matt's greasy hair. "You're an open book to me. That's why you're my boy."

"I want to be."

"My boy?"

Matt nodded.

"Then you accept my conditions?"

"I never wanted to leave," Matt confessed. "Every time I told myself to stay."

Alec knew that but it wasn't enough. "I need to hear you say it, Matt."

"I'm your boy and I'll always stay with you. I love you, Daddy Bear."

They both shivered in unison.

Alec held Matt to his heart. "That's all I needed to hear."

He rocked Matt gently and after a while, Matt's breathing deepened, and Alec realized he'd fallen asleep.

"Sleep well, little one," he murmured.

They could make love later. They had all the time in the world.

MATT

Matt heard talking above him. He knew his Daddy and the other was Harry. Unsurprising as the unofficial medic of the family, Harry would have wanted to check him over.

"How is he?" Harry said.

"Mine."

Matt buried a sleepy smile against Alec's chest.

"I asked how he is, not who he belongs to," Harry grumbled. "I'm not stupid."

"I'm sorry," Alec said. "I haven't had a chance to check him over yet. I'll give him a bath later."

"He's very thin."

"Too thin, but we'll put meat on his bones. I bet Lyle is already cooking up a feast for him."

Harry snorted. "Busted. He's sent Red and Jack to the barns for extra food and Gruff and PJ to the store in town. Matt won't be allowed to turn around without eating."

Alec sighed. "I still can't believe he's in my arms."

"Of course you can't," Harry agreed, his voice soft. "Is he home to stay?"

"He says so."

The pain cut through Matt like a knife. Alec didn't believe he wanted to stay.

"You don't believe him?"

Matt felt a hand stroke his hair gently.

"It's not whether I believe him, it's whether he believes it himself," Alec said.

Matt had a feeling his Daddy was talking to him.

"He loves you; you know that."

"And I love him."

"You don't say." Harry managed to convey all his brotherly contempt in three words. The Brenners were experts at that. "I think we all worked that one out."

"What did you do when Red was thinking it through?"

"Had a nervous breakdown and cried on Brad's shoulder." Harry sounded sheepish.

"I think we've all cried on Brad's shoulder. Me more than anyone recently."

"Our brother is good at that," Harry agreed.

"It's high time he found a boy of his own," Alec said.

"It is. But Brad can sort out his own love life. I'm here to talk about you and Matt."

Alec stroked Matt's head again. "We'll be fine, Harry. We just need a little time."

"You tell him that until he believes you, little brother. I'm here if he needs anything checked over. I'll leave you alone and he can pretend to wake up." Harry left with a chuckle.

As the door closed Matt raised his head, blinking sleepily. "Did you both know I was awake?"

"We've been Daddies a long time," Alec pointed out, not bothering to hide his grin. "We know when a boy is faking sleep."

"Then why didn't you say something?"

"Because we both thought you needed to hear our conversation."

"That's unfair," Matt grumbled.

Alec kissed him. "I know. Get over it. Ready for a bath?"

Matt wrinkled his nose. "More than ready. It was a long road trip." He stood, with a little help from Alec, and yawned, stretching his tired muscles. He sniffed his armpit and grimaced. "My clothes stink too."

"All your clothes you left are in my closet. Go pick something to wear.

Matt froze. "You didn't throw them away?"

"Why would I do that? I knew you were coming back."

Matt could barely breathe but Alec didn't seem to notice. "I've got all your gear from your apartment too. We cleaned it out when we realized the Feds were gonna hold onto you. Most of it is in the attic all boxed up. You should thank Jack, Red, and Aaron for that."

"You did that for me?"

"They did it for you. The boys missed their friend. They kept asking me when I was gonna get you back. I think they expected me to storm across the country and rescue you. I would have done if I'd known where you were."

"I should thank them."

"Later," Alec agreed. "First, a hot bubble bath. We can use Damien's room."

Matt groaned at the thought. "I can't wait."

It was odd being in Damien and Vinny's room now it was empty. Alec came back into the bedroom from starting the tub and caught Matt glancing around. "Gruff and Lyle will move in at some point. They're never going to use their cabin. Lyle loves this place too much. I think it will end up being a foster home." He placed a finger over his lips.

"Don't tell them I told you that. It's still in the early stages of negotiation."

Matt mimed zipping his mouth closed. Of all the things that could happen to the big cabin, filling it full of foster kids was the least surprising. Lyle was born to take care of people in need.

"What about you and Brad?"

"We'll move out and give them space. There's a cabin waiting for us. I just never wanted to move into it alone."

"There's a home for the two of us?" Matt asked.

In his head, he'd known there had to be at some point. All of the brothers had designed their own cabin, but he'd never asked, never wanted to commit.

"It's next to Jake and Aaron's and we have an office too, to save us from driving to town. Damien had words about us spending so much time away from home. You know what he's like. I like the office," Alec admitted. "It's got a view of the mountain and I see Harry and Red riding past with the horses. Come on, into the tub."

Matt threw off his clothes and left them in a pile, not sure what to do with them. He followed Alec into the bathroom. Alec held out his hand and helped him into the bath. It was hot, almost too hot, taking his breath away, but it was just as he loved it. Alec knew that. His Daddy knew everything about him.

Alec rolled up the sleeves of his flannel shirt, exposing his forearms covered with a layer of chestnut hair. Matt quietly drooled at the sight. He'd dreamed about those arms around him every night.

"Tip your head back, boy. I'm going to wash your hair." Alec reached over for the shampoo in a purple dinosaur bottle. All the bottles were for boys like Matt.

Matt did as he was told and closed his eyes, sighing in

pleasure as hot water tipped over his head. This was what he had missed for far too long.

After his bath, Matt stared at himself in the mirror. He barely recognized himself now that Alec had shaved him. He was thin, all his ribs prominent now. It wasn't that the Feds hadn't given him food. It was boring but adequate. He just hadn't felt much like eating the whole time he was away.

He rubbed his smooth jaw, feeling almost naked for a moment without his beard. "I thought about keeping my beard, but the minute I saw your face I knew you hated it."

"I did," Alec agreed. "I like my boys smooth."

"And the rest of me?" Matt waved at his body hair.

Alec had never made a big deal out of his light chest hair or thicker pubes. But this time Alec hummed.

"We'll deal with that. We'll take our time."

Matt cocked his head to regard him. "You're going to shave all of me?"

Alec gave him a wicked smile as he tapped the end of the razor. "You'll learn what it's like to have a Daddy, my boy. You do as I say."

"I…" Matt trailed off and shut his mouth. He'd always wanted to do what Alec ordered, but he'd rarely allowed himself the luxury of giving into his desires.

Alec smoothed his thumb along Matt's cheek. "We'll work it out together, Matty. You and me."

"Is that what you're going to call me? Matty?"

"Just when we're alone."

Matt licked his lips. "Maybe you could call me that when we join in the playroom. If they let me?"

He had been in the playroom a few times, but he didn't know if he'd be welcome anymore.

"I'll call you Matty whenever it's right for you," Alec said.

"It's time we went downstairs, isn't it?"

Matt didn't want to face the family, but he knew it had to be done.

Alec nodded. "Get it over and done with and you can start building bridges."

They dressed quickly in sweats and hoodies and shoved their feet in old slippers.

"I promise you I won't let you go," Alec said as they left the bedroom and entangled his fingers with Matt's.

"Thank you, Daddy."

As they stepped into the kitchen, the conversation died around the table and Matt clutched a little tighter onto Alec's hand. His Daddy did not let him go as he promised.

No one moved. Tears stung Matt's eyes. Did no one want to welcome him home?

9

Alec held tightly to Matt's smaller hand, feeling it shake. His boy needed to know his Daddy had his back. If he could have avoided this he would, but this meeting, or was it confrontation, had to take place at some point if Matt was to live here.

He wasn't going to threaten his brothers, but if Matt wasn't welcome here, then Alec would take his boy and find somewhere else to make their home. His family was important, but Matt was his life.

Alec waited as they all stared at each other. No one said a word and he felt Matt cower. He slid an arm around Matt's shoulders, ready to lead him away.

Then Lyle got to his feet and walked over, enfolding Matt in his arms. "Welcome back, Matt. I've missed you."

Alec let Lyle embrace Matt, but he was ready to claim his boy. Matt was rigid, then he relaxed and gave Lyle a tentative hug, enfolding the smaller boy in his arms. Alec was more than relieved. Matt and Lyle had been friends for most of their lives. If Lyle had rejected him, Matt would have been destroyed.

"Your Daddy missed you so much," Lyle whispered in Matt's ear. "Don't leave him again."

Alec held his breath as he waited for Matt's response, but his boy nodded.

"I'm here to stay, if I'm allowed."

"You're staying with me, wherever we live," Alec growled.

There. He'd made his position clear to his brothers. He saw Damien flinch and Harry's eyes narrow into slits. He fixed each brother and saw them nod one by one. He would leave if his boy wasn't welcome.

There was one person whose gaze he avoided.

Then Jack was at Lyle's back waiting for his turn. One by one the boys approached, and Alec could see the tension drain from Matt's expression. But there was still one boy left at the table.

Brad bounded over and hugged him. "I'll cut your hair soon, yeah?"

Brad did the whole family's hair, a hangover from no stylist in the town willing to do business with the brothers.

Alec held back a smile as Matt nodded against his shoulder. He hadn't had it cut since before the Feds took him and it was out of control. Matt had always been fussy who tackled his hair, but now maybe he wouldn't care so much.

Then Brad was hauled back and his other brothers hugged Matt, swallowing him up in their beefy embrace. PJ virtually swallowed Matt whole. He whispered something in Matt's ear, who nodded, but Alec didn't hear what it was. He would have to ask Matt later.

That left only Damien and Vinny sitting at the table.

Alec knew Damien wouldn't move until Vinny did. He might have been the eldest brother, but the small boy held the power in their relationship. Damien would never betray Vinny's trust.

Vinny stared down at the table, then pushed back his chair and stalked over to Matt, Rexy playing around his feet. Alec held his breath. What was Vinny going to say to him?

"Why did Rogerson treat you like the rest of us?" Once upon a nightmare, they'd all called him the CEO. But that gave him power and status.

Matt sighed. "He never wanted a son or a family. We were inconvenient. But he couldn't bring himself to kill me. He sent me away so he didn't have to deal with me."

"When did you find out?"

"When I was eighteen. I thought they were disappearing me but they transported me to a different theme park and told me I was a Greencoat. When I asked why they said I was Rogerson's son."

"Why didn't you save us?" Vinny demanded.

The kitchen was quiet waiting for Matt's answer, even Rexy had stopped trying to attract Vinny's attention and sat quietly at his feet.

"Because the Greencoats gave me a warning. If I went to the authorities, they would kill every last child."

"Christ," PJ muttered.

Alec wanted to be sick. He knew from Matt's nightmares but hearing it said in the light of day made it worse.

"They had plans to start over if anyone threatened them," Matt continued. "They used to let me know they were watching me."

Vinny crossed his arms over his chest. "How?"

Matt shivered. "You really don't want to know."

"Tell me," Vinny insisted.

But then Jack spoke up. "Little brother, believe me when I say Matt is right. You really don't want to know."

He, Aaron, and Red had found the photos in Matt's apartment. Photos of the disappeared, delivered to Matt week in, week out, until he ran away. A warning from his father.

Vinny looked as if he were about to protest, but Damien came over and squeezed Vinny's shoulder.

"Listen to them, my boy."

Vinny glowered at Matt. "We thought you were dead." We, being him and Lyle. "Even when we met you again, you didn't admit to being George."

Matt held out his hands and waited until finally Vinny took them. "I thought you were safer if I kept my mouth shut. I didn't know if you'd remembered me at first."

"I never forgot you," Lyle said. "I never forgot any of the boys who disappeared. But you were my friend."

"Lyle told me you couldn't cook at all, but you were so good with the horses," Gruff said. "He also told you about Daddies and littles."

Lyle shot him a sweet smile. "You remembered that."

Gruff tugged Lyle against him. "I remember everything you told me."

Alec's heart clenched for a moment as he watched Lyle seem to melt against him. Would he ever have that easy relationship with Matt? Then he saw Matt staring at him with a needy expression and knew his boy was begging him to take over. He reeled Matt into his arms and Matt sighed, burying his face against his chest.

The family gathering around them was overwhelming. Even Alec found it too much. He caught Jake's eyes and nodded at the table. Jake gave a brief nod.

"Give them space, guys. Matt, are you hungry?"

"Starving," Matt confessed.

"Leave it to me," Lyle said, bouncing over to the stove, Rexy following him, hopeful of scraps.

"Traitor," Vinny muttered as he watched his dog.

The situation between him and Matt still wasn't resolved, but the boy had to know that the family wanted Matt here.

Vinny huffed as he turned back to face Matt. "Give me time, okay?"

Matt nodded and Alec breathed a little easier. It wasn't resolved but maybe Vinny would come round with time. It was the most he and Matt could ask for. Alec was relieved he and Matt weren't facing a long trip down the mountain road to find somewhere else to live. It would gut him to have to leave his family. But he'd do it, for Matt.

As they ate the chicken and mac and cheese, Matt shoveled it in faster than Alec had seen him eat before.

"Didn't they feed you?" Jack asked.

"Not like Lyle's food," Matt muttered. "I've dreamed about eating this."

"My boy is a great cook," Gruff said proudly, and Lyle melted into his side.

"I love cooking for the family and Vinny is just as good."

"You're lucky to have found us," Vinny agreed.

Matt turned to look at Alec who was on his left and gave him a hard stare. "Don't get any ideas about me cooking. It isn't going to happen."

Alec quirked a smile at him. "You've eaten my food enough times. You know I can cook."

"This is true." Matt thought about it. "I'd forgotten that."

Red pursed his lips. "Why don't you work with Harry and the horses?"

"Maybe he doesn't want to," Harry said chidingly. "Not if he spent years being forced to do it."

Matt shook his head. "It's not that." He blushed as everyone turned to him. "I knew if I started doing anything on the farm, I'd never have the courage to put space between me and Alec. Working somewhere else gave me a reason not to stay." He leaned over and entangled his fingers with Alec's. "I'm sorry, Daddy. I should have listened to my heart."

Alec's heart raced at the love and sorrow in Matt's eyes. He held Matt's hand, staring at their entwined fingers. "I thought I'd never persuade you."

Gruff coughed. "Lyle said you were some kind of horse whisperer."

"They liked me. The horses, I mean. I liked being outside and the Greencoats left me alone mostly. None of them wanted to do hard, physical work."

"So how did you end up working for a realtor?" Aaron asked.

Matt grimaced. "It's not a story I want to share." He shoved food in his mouth as if to end the conversation.

Alec squeezed Matt's thigh. Unlike the rest of them, he knew the answer, but he didn't care. His boy was his now. He caught Jack and Aaron exchanging glances. They caught his glower and leaned into their Daddies.

PJ started a rumbling complaint about Lyle not saving any mac and cheese for him, which of course made all the brothers yell at him. PJ winked at Alec who gave him a grateful smile.

Matt glanced at him as they relaxed around the table. "I

never thought I'd have this again. I dreamed about being here."

"Thank you for coming back to me." Alec kissed the top of his head. "Thank you for agreeing to stay."

MATT

He leaned into Alec as they climbed the stairs together. "Do you think Vinny will ever forgive me?"

"I think he already has. He just doesn't want to admit it. Vinny is very young still. He's working through his emotions."

"He's lucky to have Damien."

Alec grunted. "I think we've all ended up with boys who complement us. Can you imagine Vinny and PJ together?"

Matt snorted at the idea. "They'd kill each other."

"It would be a nightmare. Vinny nearly killed PJ for the way he treated Damien. PJ had to work hard to make it up to both of them."

"You think you and I match?"

Alec took a moment to answer. "I think we do. Unlike all the others we're friends too. We've worked together, and you trust me."

Matt raised an eyebrow as they walked into Alec's bedroom. *Their* bedroom now, Alec had made that very clear. "Where do you get that idea from?"

"You came back to me."

"I did. I wanted to come home so many times over the past six months."

"Home. You never called it that before."

"I never dared let myself believe this could be my home."

Alec stopped and Matt found himself looking up into Alec's blue eyes.

"This is your home, here in my arms. You can live anywhere you like, but you've always been home here." Alec took one of Matt's hands and pressed it to his heart.

Matt swallowed hard and nodded. He knew that. He'd always known that, but hearing Alec speak it out loud was breathtaking.

"Alec, I love you."

"I'm your Daddy," Alec corrected.

"Daddy, I love you," Matt amended quickly.

"You and me. Forever now."

"What if they come after me again?"

Matt didn't have to explain, his Daddy understood.

"They won't. The Feds have gotten what they want from you and every single Greencoat is now behind bars."

"That sounds unlikely," Matt said dubiously. "I know some escaped."

"The Feds are convinced they've gotten them all."

Matt grimaced. He didn't want to contradict his Daddy, but these guys were wily bastards, which is why they'd gotten away with abusing so many kids over the years.

Alec tugged him closer. "Baby, you'll be with me. You'll be safe. I promise you."

"You're gonna keep me locked up here?" He felt bad when Alec flinched. "I'm sorry, Daddy."

Alec pressed a kiss on his temple. "I should think about what I'm saying around you guys."

"You don't have to treat me like I'm fragile," Matt assured him. "I'm not."

"You're precious to me, my boy, and I want you to know that. But now I want to forget about the outside world and my brothers and take you to bed."

Matt could drown in his Daddy's blue eyes. He was so distracted, he almost forgot what Alec was saying. Then he focused. "God, yes, please." He wanted to have his Daddy's cock buried in him to the root.

"On the bed," Alec ordered.

Matt flung himself on the unmade bed, promising himself he would change the sheets before they went to sleep. Alec never made the bed. It was one of the things that drove Matt crazy, but he just made the bed every day and kept the peace because he loved his Daddy.

His mouth went dry as he watched his lover strip off his clothes. He'd not forgotten the innate beauty in Alec's muscular form, his broad shoulders, slim waist, and long, muscular legs, and that mouth-watering cock Matt had sucked so many times, rising to meet him. He wasn't as bulky or as large as some of his brothers. Alec didn't have the physical job that PJ or Harry had. But he was muscular enough to make Matt drool, desperate to run his hands over Alec's body.

"You're staring at me," Alec murmured.

"You're worth staring at," Matt challenged.

Alec leaned over Matt's body and gazed in his eyes. "I'm gonna suck you, my sweet boy, until you're begging me to let you come, then I'm gonna bury my dick inside you."

"I don't need the play-by-play," Matt said breathlessly. "I'm more of a show, not tell, kind of guy."

"You want me to show you what I'm going to do, not talk about it."

"Exactly," Matt agreed, wriggling up to encourage Alec to get going.

Alec made a snorting noise and sat up, his ass pressed against Matt's hardening dick.

Matt chuckled and tried to push up. "You're a mean Daddy."

"I hope so," Alec chuckled, "or my reputation is wasted.

He wriggled down Matt's body until he was sitting on his legs and dragged Matt's sweats down. Matt arched his back and raised his rump as far as possible, not easy when there was a furry bear sitting on him. But his cock sprang free and thumped on his belly, leaving a sticky glistening streak in his body hair.

Alec licked his lips. "I have been waiting to do this for so long."

"Suck me, Daddy," Matt begged.

"Willingly," Alec said and bent to lick from root to tip.

Matt howled at the first touch. He had a feeling he wouldn't last long, his Daddy's mouth was too good. His dreams from the past six months of Alec's mouth on him were a pale imitation of the real thing. He clutched at Alec's hair, trying to guide him but Alec wasn't having any of it. Apparently, this was his rodeo and his boy had to lie there and be driven slowly out of his mind with pleasure.

Matt looked at his glistening cock slipping in and out of Alec's mouth. "So good, so good," he crooned.

Alec reached out and fumbled for the lube on the night-stand. Matt frowned at the sight of the half-used bottle.

Alec must have caught his expression because he said, "I've been jacking off at the thought of you coming home. I've never been with anyone else since the day we met, sweet boy."

That was an admission Matt hadn't expected. "You haven't?"

They'd known each other for a few years and a long time before they'd finally tumbled into bed together. Pre Lyle, Alec and his brothers weren't known for their celibacy.

Matt furrowed his brow. "You really haven't fucked anyone since we met, Daddy Bear?"

"Only you. I only ever wanted you."

Alec punctuated his sentence with one finger running from behind Matt's taut balls to his hole. Matt groaned and spread his legs as wide as he could, hampered by Alec sitting on him. Alec ran a finger around the hole.

"I haven't...since we did last time," Matt confessed.

"I'll go easy," Alec said.

Matt clutched onto Alec's arm. "I haven't fucked anyone once I knew we were serious, once everything started to happen."

Alec nodded. Matt checked his expression. He didn't seem angry that Matt couldn't make the same confession as him. But Alec bent down and gave him a toe-curling kiss, only raising his head to murmur, "Thank you for telling me."

He guessed that was the condom talk too. They'd given up on condoms once they realized they were it for each other, even when Matt was running away all the time.

"I need you inside me," Matt begged.

They'd lost the momentum with the discussion and Matt's erection had flagged a little, but one sweep of Alec's wicked tongue had it standing to attention again. Matt groaned and Alec gave a wicked chuckle as he pushed inside Matt's hole with one finger.

Matt clutched onto Alec's biceps. Sweet Jesus, he was going to come apart at the seams if Alec didn't get inside him soon. But Alec took his time, crooning to Matt in his ear, each rumbling word as if it were linked straight to Matt's cock.

One finger became two, two became three, three... " Daddy, get the hell on with it. I'm not a blushing virgin."

Alec raised an eyebrow.

"I'm sorry," Matt said contritely.

"So you should be," Alec said sternly. "I should put you in a cage for days."

Knowing his orgasm was on the line, Matt said, "I'm really sorry, Daddy."

Alec growled, but he took out his fingers and leaned over him. "I'll discipline you when we're finished."

Matt held back a gasp of excitement. They hadn't really ventured into discipline and control. They hadn't had time because they'd been saving the goddamn world. He hoped Alec would spank his ass hard until it was rosy-red, and he could admire it in the mirror.

But he didn't have time to think as Alec put Matt's legs over his shoulders and, pushing into Matt's hole, drove into the root. Matt yelled, and Alec hesitated.

"Don't stop, don't stop," Matt begged. "I need."

"What do you need?"

"I need you."

Alec wrapped his arms around Matt's thighs and shoved in harder. "Like this?"

"More!" It was a demand, an order, but for once, Alec didn't tell him off.

Alec drove into him again and again, their eyes locked on each other. Matt's orgasm caught him before he'd even had time to think about it. He yelled as he came hard, cum covering his belly and chest. In the back of his mind, he heard Alec coming too, filling up his ass, making him inexorably Alec's forever.

10

ALEC

Matt stared at him, his mouth open. "You've got to be joking."

"Don't make me say it again." Alec held back a sigh. He wanted to get the discipline portion over with so they could enjoy the rest of the evening with the family. Now it seemed they were going to spend it in a standoff, glaring at each other. This was a fight Matt was not going to win and the sooner he realized that the better.

"I've just remade the bed," Matt pointed out.

"And now you take the punishment."

"You want me to stand in the corner?" Matt scowled at the corner and then back at him.

"I told you there would be a punishment for being rude to me," Alec said calmly.

"I thought you'd spank my butt."

Alec watched Matt shiver and wiggle his ass at the idea. "You enjoy it far too much. It's not a punishment."

"But—"

Alec folded his arms. "Fifteen minutes in the corner."

"You said ten!"

"Twenty minutes."

Matt opened his mouth, then shut it, and opened it again. At Alec's eyebrow raise, he stomped over to the corner and pressed his nose to the wall.

"That's so unfair," he muttered.

"Twenty-five."

At this rate, they'd be going nowhere all evening. Alec sat down in his chair, so he could keep an eye on his boy, and pulled out his phone to check the time and catch up on business. He scrolled through his emails, noting a few he needed to talk to Jake about. He and Jake needed to catch up soon to discuss the new business arrangements. They'd been so busy for two years with a steady income, it was strange and worrying to think they would have to start looking for new business.

Josh Cooper had suggested a change in direction for them, but he needed to talk about it with Jake. He and his brother had enjoyed being small-town PIs. They dealt with things local to the mountain, and most of the time it worked. Of course, the Kingdom Mountain theme park had been local and unfolded into a country-wide nightmare.

He hoped never to be involved in something like that again. He was a small-town boy.

Alec tapped out a message to Jake.

We need to talk tomorrow.

The response was almost instantaneous.

Problem?

No. Just the future.

Cooper's offer worrying you?

Alec rolled his eyes. His brother knew him far too well.

No. Yes. Maybe.

We'll talk with our boys too.

That was a good idea. Aaron and Matt would have a lot to say. Matt had been involved from the beginning and Aaron had struggled to find his way with a new job. He'd wanted to see if he could get his old job back at the Tin Bar, but as he was underage despite what his documents said, Jake had put the kybosh on that. Aaron protested constantly: but Jake ignored him. Alec could learn a lot from the way his brother handled his highly-strung boy.

Thanks bro.

Got your back A.

Alec's eyes prickled with unexpected emotion. His brothers were the best and Jake especially.

They had about ten minutes to go before the end of the punishment. Alec contemplated stopping it now, but he was a strict Daddy and didn't dish out punishments for no reason. He stuck to them too. His boys needed to know their boundaries.

He clicked through the news headlines. Any interest in the theme parks had long since faded away and Matt's release by the Feds hadn't generated any news coverage, even locally. Alec wondered if Cooper had anything to do with that.

Matt hadn't made a move since he'd voiced his complaint, but his back radiated tension. Alec wondered for a moment how to end this. Matt was the longest almost-relationship he'd had with a boy. It hadn't bothered him before. He and Jake were always traveling with their business. But now Matt was his and they were going to have to learn about each other, go beyond the fun to the serious deep diving into a 24/7 Daddy/boy relationship. Would they survive it?

Just the thought of not being able to last made his guts tighten. They'd survived so much. They'd learn to be a couple.

He glanced at his watch. "Come here, Matt." He made his voice gentle. Matt rushed over to him without hesitation and climbed into his lap, burying his face into the curve of Alec's neck.

"I'm sorry," Matt muttered.

Alec held him close. "These are the things we need to talk about, my boy."

"How we negotiate our relationship?"

"Exactly."

Matt raised his head, and when he looked at Alec, his eyes red-rimmed, Alec realized he'd been crying. His heart clenched at the idea that he'd made his boy hide his crying. But before Alec could speak, Matt did.

"I've never been in a relationship before. I'm worried I'll fuck this up, Daddy." He scrunched up his nose. "Damn."

"I'll put two dollars in the jar," Alec said with resignation, "but clean up your mouth."

"Yes, Daddy Bear."

That was way too faux innocent, but Alec would take it. He was too tired to fight.

"We'll negotiate our relationship the way we do everything else, Matt. Together."

Matt regarded him for a moment, then nodded. "That sounds good. Scary, but good."

Alec brushed his thumb along Matt's now smooth cheekbone. "We will work it out, sweetheart. We always have."

"I was just too scared to see it," Matt agreed.

"You weren't the only one. Let's go talk to the others. I need a snack. We've been busy." He gave Matt a wink who laughed and bounced off him.

As he and Matt went downstairs, hand-in-hand, Alec wondered just how much negotiating they'd have to do. Matt had a lifetime of hiding his true self. Would he be able to open up to Alec? Or would he struggle?

"You're thinking hard," Matt said, glancing at him.

"I am," he admitted. "It's nothing important."

"Uh-huh." Matt shot him a skeptical look. "Because that's so convincing."

Alec stopped near the bottom step. "Are you asking for a smacked bottom?"

Matt's shiver was very satisfying, then he poked his butt out. The move was spoiled by the fact he slipped and would have fallen down the remaining stairs if Alec hadn't grabbed ahold of his biceps and pulled his boy against him.

"Why, Daddy Bear, what strong arms you have," Matt said breathlessly.

"We've done Red Riding Hood already," Alec said.

Matt furrowed his brow. "You're right. We have. Dang, what's left for us? Cinderfella?"

Alec shook his head. "You're no princess at the ball and I'm definitely not Prince Charming."

"Rapunzel?"

"Done."

Matt thought for a moment. "Jack's done, so is Snow White. You're no Ugly Duckling. What about Beauty & the Beast?"

"You're calling me a beast?" Alec asked, because what other part could he play?

But Matt didn't return his smile and Alec's faded. Matt took Alec's hand and led them downstairs, then he turned and placed his hands over Alec's muscled chest.

"You're the beauty and I'm the beast."

"No—"

"I've always been the beast," Matt insisted. "I've had this ugliness inside me forever, hiding who I am. It's eaten me up inside and I was too knotted up inside to realize you were my Beauty, the one to set me free from the curse."

Alec frowned. He didn't like what Matt was saying. His boy had been as much a victim as the other boys. He wasn't treated any better just because his father had been a monster.

"I was scared when you asked me to get involved. I knew it was dangerous for me, yet it was the best thing I could have done. Each child we've rescued, each theme park closed, has been like a petal falling from the rose." He looked up into Alec's blue eyes. "The curse was like the rose. It had to die to set me free."

Finally, Alec nodded, then he gave a wicked grin. "Does this mean my family plays the household servants?"

Matt barked out a laugh. "We've got to have a supporting cast. Vinny is Chip. Lyle has got to be Mrs. Potts."

"Who is Gaston?" Alec asked.

"It's got to be PJ."

"You know they're never going to forgive you for this."

"They never have to know," Matt assured him before they walked into the kitchen. "This is a secret between you and me."

"I thought we were quitting with the secrets," PJ grumbled as he walked past with Jack in his arms. "That's what got you into trouble the last time."

"These are couple secrets and they're allowed," Alec said. "Where are you going?"

"We're going to have playtime upstairs. Everyone is invited. Jack and I are gonna get the room ready."

Matt clutched onto Alec's hand. "And me? Am I invited too, Daddy PJ?" He wasn't going to take anything for granted, especially his welcome back into the family.

PJ glanced at Alec for permission who nodded, then he focused his attention on Matt. "You're family. Of course, you're joining us. Lyle is bringing drinks and snacks."

God, Alec loved his family. Matt sniffled a little and Alec drew him close to whisper in his ear. "Let's go to the ball, my boy."

MATT

He turned and ran back up the stairs, Alec on his heels. Matt headed to the playroom, but Alec tugged and pointed at what had been PJ's room.

"We needed a bigger playroom, so we've upgraded." As Matt narrowed his eyes, Alec added hastily, "I've not been in here with a boy. I waited for you."

Matt breathed easier, then a thought occurred to him. "Will you move into your cabin now?"

"We will," Alec corrected. "You need to see what you'd like to add. I'm taking my bed though. I like my bed too much to get another one."

As Alec's bed was the most comfortable thing he'd ever slept in, and he'd slept in basically a cell for the past six months. Matt wasn't arguing.

They were the first to arrive after PJ and Jack, so Alec claimed one of the big chairs with a triumphant cry and Matt snagged his favorite plushie to cuddle, a blue velour dinosaur. They snuggled in the chair and waited for the others to arrive.

Alec's arms were strong around him and Matt hadn't felt this protected since the day Alec hugged him tight and promised to wait for him before the Feds took him away.

One by one the couples arrived, the boys wearing onesies or pajamas.

"Do you want to change?" Alec asked.

Matt shook his head. He wasn't ready to be his boy yet. Too much had happened for him to relax enough.

"You let me know when you're ready," Alec murmured.

He wasn't even sure where his onesie and boy's pajamas were, although he guessed they were with the rest of his things brought from his apartment.

"Your boy clothes are in my closet."

Matt was very lucky to have a Daddy like Alec and he didn't have to explain his thoughts. Alec knew him well enough now to know what he was thinking.

Gruff and Lyle brought flasks and plates of cookies and chips. Then Lyle and Vinny headed straight for the cars. Jake brought Anna and they snuggled in another chair. Matt was relieved Aaron was still comfortable enough to be herself in front of him. Red and Jack disappeared over to one corner to play with a train set. They started bickering immediately, but everyone ignored them.

"Do you want to join them?" Alec asked.

"I've had enough of corners," Matt groused and stayed where he was.

Alec chuckled and held him as tight as he held the dinosaur.

Matt noticed Brad hadn't joined them. "Where's Brad?"

"He says this is Daddy and boy time and he shouldn't interfere," Damien said. "He's gone down to the Tin Bar as it's a Tuesday."

"We've told him he's welcome. He's family. He should be here." Harry grumbled. "But he refuses to join in."

"It's hard for him," Gruff added. "Seeing everyone happy now. It just reminds him of what he hasn't got, a boy of his own. I think he's missing that kid...um...Eric?"

Matt nodded. He'd known Brad long enough to know he'd always said he didn't want a boy. But being faced with six loved-up couples had to be hard. It had been hard enough for Alec, and they'd been kind of together from the start.

"We used to bring boys here," PJ pointed out. "He could have done that." He was faced with six pairs of eyes glaring at him, including a furious Jack. "What did I say?"

"You're an idiot, PJ," Damien huffed. "No boy wants to be reminded of the ones that came before."

"Oh." PJ turned to Jack. "They aren't important now."

"They'd better not be," Jack growled.

Everyone huffed and grumbled but a few minutes later they were back playing with the toys.

"I'm sorry I broke the mood, Daddy," Matt whispered to Alec.

"It's okay. We all want him here but know why he isn't. Even if he picked up a boy, it wouldn't be the same for him. We have our forever boys. He would feel it. Brad's a sensitive soul."

Matt nodded and settled back into Alec's arms. He felt sorry for Alec's brother. He knew how it felt to be out of place in the family. Then Alec raised his chin and kissed him, and all thoughts drained away and all he focused on was his Daddy's mouth on his.

When they broke away from their kiss, drinks and snacks were being passed around. Matt was half-hard and very flushed, but no one would worry about that. The rules of the playroom were very simple. A Daddy and his boy could do anything together except interfere with another couple.

Alec handed him a cup of hot chocolate and a cookie. Matt would have preferred a strong cup of coffee because he was flagging after an emotional day, but only the Daddies were allowed coffee in the playroom.

When Alec got involved in a discussion with Jake and Gruff, Anna smiled at him over the rim of her plastic cup. She wore a pink dress and socks with pink frills. "I'm glad you're with us again. Daddy Alec was so unhappy without you."

Matt sighed. It creased him up inside just thinking of his lonely Daddy being sad.

"Anna, what did I say about talking grown-up talk in the playroom?" Jake said chidingly, turning away from his discussion.

Anna hung her head. "I'm sorry, Daddy."

Alec looked resigned but he gave Anna a sweet smile. No one wanted to upset her. "It's all right, Daddy Jake. Anna is right. I was miserable without my boy. I'm so happy now he's with me again."

She gave him a shy smile. Anna was much shyer than Aaron.

"I'm with you forever. I'm never going to leave you now." Matt reached up to kiss and reassure him.

They kissed again and Matt sank into the feel of his Daddy's mouth on his, his bushy beard tickling Matt's smooth chin.

"Careful."

Someone took Matt's drink out of his hand. Matt didn't break the kiss, just wrapping his arm around Alec's neck.

He spent the evening in his Daddy's lap, exchanging kisses or burying his face in Alec's neck. Occasionally he talked to one of the boys but really he was content to be where he was, home in his Daddy's arms.

———

The next morning, after a night when Alec didn't let him go once, Jake and Alec showed him the new office. Matt whistled at the comfortable couches, the smart desks, and the enormous screen on one wall.

"What's that for?" Matt asked, pointing to the screen. This was new since he left them.

"We needed it when we were tracking the Greencoats." Jake flicked on the screen to show a large map of the states with clusters of green lights.

Matt furrowed his brow. "What are the green lights for?"

"It's where the Greencoats are being held," Alec said. "It replaced that map we had with pins, you remember? At one point there were green lights over the map, but we found them and made sure the cops picked them up."

Matt stared at them both. "Is this what you've been doing the past six months?"

"Me, Jake, and Aaron. Yeah." Alec shrugged. "I had to find something to do."

"Big brother wasn't going to let you come out with any of these bastards roaming the country," Jake advised him. He and Aaron were perched on an empty desk. "He didn't want to take the chance of the bastards finding you."

Matt turned to Alec. "You guys caught them all?"

"Well, the cops found some. The Feds, others. We found most of them because we had the resources to do so."

"You mean Cooper."

Alec shrugged. "He's gotta be useful for something."

Matt's lips twitched. "And my father?"

"You know they caught Rogerson three years ago." Alec raised an eyebrow. "Are you worried he's escaped or something?"

"I don't trust him not to escape and start again under a new name. It's easy to traffic vulnerable kids."

"It is," Jake agreed, "and he's a sneaky ass...criminal, but this time there are several agencies watching for any activity like it."

"And at the moment," Alec added, "he's dropped into hell somewhere. The Feds won't tell me where, but they've promised he'll never see the light of day again."

Matt hummed. He wasn't as convinced that his father wouldn't find a way to start another evil empire, but that was for another day.

"So what are you going to do now?"

"We," Alec snapped. "We. Jake and Aaron, you and me. I'm not letting you out of my sight for one second."

Matt licked his lips. "We," he agreed meekly.

Jake took over as Alec was still scowling at Matt. "We're keeping our office in town. People don't want to drive up here. You and Aaron are going to get your licenses to be a PI.

We're gonna run a local enterprise, which kept Jake and me busy before the world went to hell, and Cooper's got other work for us. We can't decide what we want to do most, so we're gonna do both. Red and Jack have expressed interest in helping us if we need it. They both need a chance to get off the mountain occasionally."

"You're thinking a family enterprise?" Matt asked. "What about the farm?"

"Life changed around us, sweet boy," Alec said. "We discovered the world needed saving by a family of Daddy brothers and their boys. We're not leaving here, just changing what we do."

Matt smiled but he was sad and guilty at heart. One of the attractions of the Brenner brothers had been their innocence. That had been lost and his father was responsible.

Alec gathered Matt into his arms. "Kingdom Mountain will always be here for us, Matt. You and me, we only have to look up and we'll see the lights twinkling for us, showing us the way home."

"I am home, Daddy. I'm in your arms."

"You're in my heart, sweet boy. You're always in my heart."

ON TO THE NEXT

From Sue Brown:

I'm almost at the end of Bearytales. It's been a sweet and a little angsty ride. Thank you for sharing the journey with me.

Enjoy a small teaser for ***Bear in Boots***, the final book in the Bearytales series

Brad

"Brad, are you in there?"

Brad held his breath and kept quiet, hoping Harry would go away.

"He's in there. He's got to be. The cabin rattled ten minutes ago," Gruff said.

Damn, Brad had forgotten about that. The explosion had been bigger than he'd anticipated.

"Maybe he's unconscious," Damien rumbled.

Brad rolled his eyes at his eldest brother's suggestion. Trust Damien to go straight to the worst-case scenario. Like

Brad would knock himself out after the experience he had with explosions.

"What are you guys doing?" Aaron asked. "Why are you all huddled around the door?"

"It's lunchtime. Lyle is cooking dinner. He sent us to find him." Harry said.

"No, he sent me," Gruff pointed out. "You lot just came along for the ride...and to get out of helping my boy."

"True," Harry agreed. "It was getting tense in there."

"If you try and tell the prince of the potato peeler that he's doing it wrong, you deserve the earbashing you received," Aaron said bluntly. He was Jake's boy and never minced his words. After years of working in the Tin Bar, he didn't suffer fools gladly. "What were you thinking?"

Brad nearly groaned out loud, clapping a hand over his mouth in case he gave himself away. Upsetting Vinny, the aforementioned prince of the potato peeler, was a really bad idea. He'd be sulking for days. Damien would be upset because his boy was sulking, and then none of them would be able to sit down and talk to him about their day. It was a thing. All the family did it. Potato time was therapy time for whoever needed it. Brad had written poems about it.

"I didn't mean to upset him," Harry protested.

"Well, you have," Damien said. "It's going to take me the rest of the day to calm him down."

"Why aren't you with him?" Aaron said pointedly.

"He told me to go away," Damien muttered. "Me. His Daddy."

"He just wants to cry on Lyle's shoulder while no one else is there to see it. You can punish him later," Aaron said. "Now hurry up and find your brother. My balls are ready to climb inside my body, it's so cold out here."

Inside the barn, Brad sighed. He didn't want to miss

lunch, his belly rumbled just at the thought, but he didn't want to eat with his brothers and their boys.

It was...hard for him now. He was lonely. How a man could be lonely in a family of thirteen men he didn't know. But Brad was. His six brothers had all found their boys and he was alone. He'd told himself it didn't matter, he'd always been happy to be lone wolf, but that was before he was faced with the reality of living with six loved-up couples.

Lately, he'd taken to hiding in his barns during the day rather than sharing the family meals, then spending his evenings in town at the Tin Bar and staying overnight at the motel. But that was lonely too and he wistfully remembered the times he and his brothers used to drink together in the bar and cause mayhem.

"Brad!" Damien bellowed.

"Careful, big man. You'll cause an avalanche," Aaron muttered. "Open the door."

"We don't do that," Harry said.

"Do what?"

"Open the door. In case he's about to blow something up. It could get messy."

This was an unspoken rule. No one interrupted Brad without warning. PJ had done it once and spent an entire summer waiting on his brother, hand and foot, as he recovered from his injuries.

"He knows we're here," Gruff pointed out. "We've been talking for long enough. He's hiding and hoping we'll go away."

Brad flinched. His baby brother was right, but he didn't have to say it out loud.

"Get out of the way."

Then the barn door was flung open. Brad stared at Aaron in the doorway, flanked by his three brothers towering over him. It looked like an advert for men's flannel shirts.

"It's lunchtime," Aaron snapped. "Are you done hiding?"

"I'm kinda busy," Brad lied. "I'll come in later."

Damien growled in exasperation. "It's a family meal. We always eat together."

They did. Brad knew this. And even Red, who struggled with the family idea, joined in. But—

Brad found himself herded out before he'd even completed the thought. Harry shut the barn door and they all headed to the big cabin.

Damien slung a meaty arm around Brad's shoulders. As the two eldest brothers they'd always been close. "You know hiding is a bad thing, right?"

He had hidden in the barns a lot when he was trying to avoid Vinny. His brothers had staged an intervention then, too.

"I didn't think anyone had noticed," Brad admitted, leaning into his older brother, just for a moment.

"We noticed," Harry said from behind him, and Gruff grunted.

"I know why you're hiding," Damien said, "and I'm sorry. It's gotta be hard for you. But I hate the thought you don't want to spend time with us."

Brad flinched. He knew his absence would be a sore point with Damien. Since the Kingdom orphanages had been closed and years had passed with the family at home, the clawing need to stay together had eased, but his big old sappy brother was always going to be the one to suffer if one of the family was away for too long.

"I'll try and spend more time with you," he muttered.

Damien hugged him closer. "Thanks."

Brad didn't need to look at him to know he was choked up. Sap.

The warmth of the kitchen was a relief. Rexy, Vinny's dog, was in his usual spot by the stove when Lyle cooked. Close enough to get anything dropped but not enough to get under Lyle's feet.

Vinny flung himself at Damien who scooped him up and took him out of the kitchen.

"Don't take too long to kiss and make up," Lyle yelled.

Brad sniffed. Whatever was in the oven smelled fabulous. "Meatloaf?"

Lyle smiled at him. "It's your favorite."

"You made this for me?"

"I did. And mashed potatoes and greens."

Brad swallowed hard. He was choked up at the thought Lyle had made a meal, especially for him. "Thanks, Lyle."

He received a sweet smile in return. "You're welcome. Now wash up and sit at the table."

Lyle was his youngest brother Gruff's boy and without a doubt, the best cook in the family. Vinny was a close second, and despite his grumbles, Jack was learning too. It didn't mean to say the brothers couldn't cook. It just meant Lyle did it better. Brad thought Lyle was even better than his mom, but she wouldn't have minded.

One by one all the brothers came in until the huge pine table was full and everyone was laughing and joking. Brad pasted a huge smile on his face and joined in. He would fake happiness if it was the last thing he did. He owed his family that.

They were about to eat when someone knocked at the kitchen door.

"Are we expecting anyone?" Gruff asked, but everyone shook their heads.

Being so far up the mountain, they usually knew who was visiting. Recently, the unknown visitors had been unwelcome, to say the least, so they let it be known that people had to message before dropping in.

"Someone answer the door before the food gets cold," PJ grumbled.

Gruff stood and Jack nudged his Daddy.

"You go too."

PJ grumbled again but he obediently followed Gruff over to the door because he'd do anything for Jack, and Damien joined them.

"You don't have to scare the living daylights out of them," Lyle murmured.

"Until we know if they're friend or foe we do," Brad said.

Gruff opened the door. "Can I help you?"

A stranger then.

"I...uh...is Bradley Brenner at home?"

It took a moment for Brad to realize they were asking for him. No one had called him by his full name in years.

"Uh..." Gruff sounded as bemused as he was. He looked over his shoulder. "Brad?"

"Who is it?" Brad asked.

A tall man peered around the three man-mountains in his way. He was young, sweet-faced, with dark brown hair and huge brown eyes blinking behind large, rimmed glasses. "Mr. Brenner?"

Brad got to his feet. "I'm Brad Brenner. I'm sorry, who are you?"

He waved at his brothers to get out of the way. They shuffled back to their seats, leaving the stranger, dressed in a jacket and jeans more suitable to warmer climates than

Kingdom Mountain in the dead of winter, shivering in the doorway.

Brad blinked. "Eric, is that you?"

The man stared at him blankly. "Uh...yes. How did you know my name?"

Read **Bear in Boots**, the final book in the Bearytales series

You can find all of Sue's books over at Amazon. Don't forget to sign up for her newsletter here.

ABOUT SUE BROWN

Cranky middle-aged author with an addiction for coffee, and a passion for romancing two guys. She loves her dog, she loves her kids, and she loves coffee; in which order very much depends on the time of day.

Come over and talk to Sue at:

Newsletter: http://bit.ly/SueBrownNews
Bookbub: https://www.bookbub.com/profile/sue-brown
TikTok: https://www.tiktok.com/@suebrownstories
Patreon: https://www.patreon.com/suebrownstories
Her website: http://www.suebrownstories.com/
Author group – Facebook: https://www.facebook.com/groups/suebrownstories/
Facebook: https://www.facebook.com/SueBrownsStories/
Email: sue@suebrownstories.com